O.

CRO\ ⸻2

BROTHERHOOD & FAMILY BEFORE ALL

By

Michelle Dups

Happy Reading!

Michelle Dups

xxx

2023

<u>DEDICATIONS</u>

This book is dedicated to every parent who has ever lost a child.

The grief of losing a child is like no other and no matter whether that child is lost in days, weeks, months, born sleeping, a teenager or an adult.

They will always be your baby!

Loved and missed but never forgotten.

May their souls rest in peace until we meet again.

THANK YOU!

Thank you for taking the time and a chance on me, I hope you enjoy reading my books as much as I enjoy writing them. Books make life a little easier to handle in these strange times.

I write what I like to read. Life is hard enough as it is, so there is little angst in my books. They all have a have happy endings, and strong family vibes with alpha males and strong females.

I am an English author so my American readers will notice a few different words used. As the series commences, I will publish a list in the front of the books. Please feel free to message me with words you are not sure about and I will add them to the list.

I hope you enjoy reading about my Crow MC family and the life they are building for themselves.

List of Characters

CROW MC

ORIGINALS - RETIRED

ALAN CROW (SHEP) m. KATE CROW

Children: KANE (REAPER) AVYANNA (AVY)

ROBERT DAVIES (DOG) m. MAGGIE DAVIES

Children: LIAM (DRACO) MILO (ONYX) IRISH TWINS

BELLAMY (BELLA)

THEO WRIGHT (THOR)

Children: MARCUS (ROGUE) BELLONA (NONI)

JACOB OWENS (GUNNY) (First wife deceased) p. BEVERLY

Children: DRAKE (DRAGON) Adopted: ALEC

JONES - DECEASED

ROMAN - DECEASED

CROW MC

1st GENERATION – ORIGINALS

KANE CROW (REAPER) **PRESIDENT** p.ABBY

Children: SAM, BEN, BREN, ELLIE

LIAM DAVIES (DRACO) **VP**

MILO DAVIES (ONYX) **SGT AT ARMS** p. ANDREA (REA) LAWSON

Children: MILA

MARCUS WRIGHT (ROGUE) **ROAD CAPTAIN**

DRAKE OWENS (DRAGON) TREASURER

AVYANNA CROW

BELLONA WRIGHT (NONI)

BELLAMY DAVIES (BELLA)

CROW MC

NEW BROTHERS

KEVIN LAWLESS (HAWK) **ENFORCER**

ALAN GOODE (NAVY) **ENFORCER**

SAMUEL ADAMS (BULL) **MEDIC**

PROSPECTS

WILLIAM ADAMS (SKINNY)

TRISTAN JOHNSON (BLAZE)

ANDREW SMITH (BOND)

AMUN JONES (CAIRO)

OTHER CHARACTERS

LEE MASTERS – GYM OWNER

CARLY MASTERS – GRANDDAUGHTER

OLD MAN JENSEN – OWNER OF THE FARM NEXT DOOR TO CROW MANOR

MOLLY JENSEN – GRANDDAUGHTER

JULIA WALKER – TEACHER AT THE SECONDARY SCHOOL

O'SHEA'S

OLD MAN O'SHEA – NONI'S EX-FATHER-IN-LAW

RHETT - NONI'S EX-HUSBAND (IN PRISON)

LIAM

JOHNNY

ADAM

ANDY   YOUNGEST BROTHER SENT TO IRELAND TO FAMILY

MC Owned Businesses

TRICKSTER CAFE

CROW INVESTMENTS

STICKY TRICKY BAKERY

CORVUS PUB

CROW GARAGE

CRAWAN GYM

RAVEN ROOST CAMPSITE – coming soon

List of English Words

Twatwaffle – an idiot – general insult

Yum Yums - It's basically a deep-fried croissant, drenched in icing. They are so delicious.

Trackies/Trackie bottoms – Sweatpants

Trainers – sneakers/running shoes

Wanker – umm self-explanatory I think.

Onyx and Rea's Songs

Perfect by Ed Sheeran

Little Lion Man by Mumford & Sons

NOTE FROM THE AUTHOR

Hello, my lovely readers!

A little note from me on this book. This book talks about miscarriage and infant loss. Please don't read this book if either of these are sensitive subjects for you.

It's a tough subject, and to this day, it's not often spoken about. However, this is a personal subject. A Beta reader brought to my attention that some readers may be angry with Rea for not letting Onyx's family know. She had never had an experience like this, for which I am eternally grateful, as I wouldn't wish it on anyone.

After I explained that I had written this with personal experience, and I know that for the first three months after it happened, I hardly spoke to anyone. It was hard enough just getting out of bed and getting on with my day. I didn't tell the rest of the family for about six months, and it was a good sixteen months before I started feeling like myself, and that was with the support of my husband, my mum, and my two children, keeping me busy. It's still a painful subject, and to this day, we rarely discuss it, although I don't shy away from the subject when it's brought up.

The graveyard scene was hard to write, and I cried all the way through it. It was actually pretty cathartic. I hope I have handled this sympathetically, and that it is still an enjoyable read.

Their story is so much more than the loss of their baby, and I hope you love their second-chance romance and catching up with the rest of the Crows as much as I did.

Much love,

Michelle

CHAPTER 1

ONYX

FEANNAG HOSPITAL A&E

MAY 2003

Grimacing, I moved my leg on the bed, groaning in pain as I caught the ice pack before it fell off my ankle. I had taken a fall off my bike when a car got close enough to clip my back tyre. Luckily, I hadn't been going more than thirty miles per hour at the time, so the damage done was minimal. A bit of gravel rash and a sprained ankle. My bike, on the other hand, was totalled. The vehicle that hit me had driven off without stopping. Strangers had stopped and called for an ambulance, where I had a free ride to our local A&E to get checked out.

We knew there would be blowback from blowing up the ACES meth labs, and it was partly my fault for being caught unawares. Reaper had ordered us to only ride out in pairs, but I'd needed some quiet time.

Between the kids, the women, and my brothers all at the manor or in the clubhouse, there wasn't time to just think. Not that thinking was helping either, other than bringing back memories of the woman I'd hurt so badly, I didn't think she would ever be able to forgive me.

I was contemplating having one of the nurses call Draco or Noni to come and get me when I caught a glimpse of said woman who had held my heart since the age of fourteen.

I sat on the bed and watched her like a man dying of thirst, and she was the last drop of water on this earth.

God, she was beautiful.

Even after having a baby, she was still slim. The only difference I could see, and to me, it was a tick in the plus column, was that her hips were wider, and her breasts were fuller. Her hair was still a white blonde, a colour she hated but was a genetic feature passed down from her mother.

I knew from memory that her eyes were dark, almost emerald green, and she had a row of freckles across her cheeks and nose that she'd hated but I'd loved.

To me, she was just as beautiful as the day she had walked into our classroom so many years ago. I remembered it as clearly as if it was yesterday.

I had been sitting laughing and joking at the back of the class with Reaper, Draco, Rogue and Dragon while we waited for the teacher to come in.

It was as if I felt the air change and get sucked out of the room. I looked up just as the door opened, and our history teacher entered with a new girl. I remember feeling like I had been hit in the stomach. I couldn't catch a breath as I watched her nod at the teacher's words, and he pointed to the desk next to me. Her head had lifted, and our eyes connected. From that day, I was hooked.

My only thought was 'Mine'. I knew then this girl was it for me. She'd held my eyes until she came to a stop at my desk, motioning for me to move my legs so she could get past. I let her through, and she sat down.

"Milo," I said, holding my hand out to her in introduction.

"Andrea, but I go by Rea."

She shook my hand shyly. I introduced her to my brother and cousins, who hadn't even realised she had sat down until I introduced them.

"Mine," I muttered to Draco as soon as I saw he was about to try to charm her.

He raised an eyebrow in surprise, but I held his gaze before looking at each of them in turn.

To say they were surprised was an understatement. I wasn't a social kid and didn't need tons of friends. I was happiest in the company of my brother and cousins.

Rea and I were inseparable from that day on. From finishing school and Rea heading to college and then University to me joining the military. We had adults worrying about us getting too serious and not seeing other people, but we had a plan.

It was a good plan, and it worked. We saw each other whenever we could and wrote letters daily.

Until it all changed. I was the cause of all the pain and unhappiness we both suffered.

My company had been on patrol and had been hit by a bomb. I remember the cloying smoke, the screams of my teammates, and the scent of blood in the air. Out of a team of eight, only two of us survived that day.

It was a dark time for me, and it only got darker when I attended the funeral of my fallen teammates while on medical leave.

One of the widows lost it and had fallen apart at his graveside. I had gone to pay my respects and her words to this day were like a slap.

"I hope you don't have a wife or girlfriend waiting for you because I can tell you that this is cruel to us. Waiting for the call to tell us that you're dead."

Her face had been streaked with tears, and the agony in her voice had shaken me.

I had left the cemetery and sought comfort in Rea, who, as always, welcomed me with open arms and gave me the comfort I needed.

But as I lay in bed that night listening to her breathing softly next to me, her naked length pressed against me, I wondered if some of what that widow had said was true. I had just signed up for another four years.

Was I being selfish?

I asked her to wait for me when anything could have happened in those years, and Rea would have waited for me for nothing. I couldn't shake the guilt that I was somehow holding her back from living her life waiting for me.

When I had brought this up with Reaper and the guys, they had cautioned me to wait until I wasn't grieving my teammates and not to do anything rash. They wanted me to speak to Rea and get her opinion, but I couldn't. I knew she would stick with me.

On my next leave, I concocted a plan using Rebecca, a girl from school who had hated Rea. I laid out my plan and should have stopped when Rebecca asked me three times if I was sure this was what I wanted. For someone who hated Rea as much as she did, but was still hesitant to go forward with the plan should have been a red flag. But as usual, I was committed once I got a thought in my head.

We posed pictures, making it look as if we were having sex, and I paid Rebecca a thousand pounds to show them to Rea and make her believe that I had been cheating on her. It was the only way I knew to really break her and have her accept that we were over. I would rather this than the pain of maybe one day her getting notification of my death.

It worked.

The devastation on her face when I showed up at the flat she shared with flatmates haunts me to this day. And had I known then what I know now after the beating Dragon gave me last month, I would have done anything I had to, to show her that I was full of shit.

I had spent the rest of my leave blackout drunk. When Draco found me three days later, he'd beaten the crap out of me when he found out what I'd done.

A few years later, Noni told us that Rea was getting married. My heart felt like it fractured in my chest. I had gone on a spiral that, to this day, I didn't know how I didn't get myself killed. Until then, the only woman I had been with was Rea, but after hearing about her engagement, I fucked anything with a pulse. I wasn't picky. I was careless on missions until it was known that I would go into any situation, anywhere, with no worries about whether I made it out or not.

Then a few years later, I got news of her divorce, and it was like a switch flipped. I stopped being an idiot, cleaned up my act, and started seeing a therapist during my leave. They helped me to understand my reasoning, during my grief, why I had done what I had.

I never thought I would see her again, and I was content to live my life with my brothers and family. But I knew a relationship, or a family wasn't in the cards for me. And then, on a night out at a local club the next town over, I'd looked up and saw a familiar pair of green eyes watching me from across the room. But before I could approach her, the shit had hit the fan with Noni's ex-in-laws, and Bull had gotten stabbed.

Rea had come back to the house with us to sew him up and had then dropped the bomb that she had a daughter.

It had hit me hard that she had someone else's child, and she had made it clear that she didn't want anything to do with me. Dragon had driven her home and then came back and had given me a good beat down, only to give me hope when he told me what she had named her daughter.

I was pulled out of my memories by the curtain being pulled around my bed and looked up into those familiar green eyes.

"Milo," she acknowledged.

"Sugar," I replied, getting a growl from her, making me grin.

"It's Dr Lawson, not Sugar," Rea muttered.

She flipped through my chart and made a few notes before gently checking my ankle.

"You're lucky. Your x-ray doesn't show a break. It's just severely sprained. You need to keep it elevated as much as possible and ice it regularly to get the swelling down. You should see an improvement in a couple of weeks and should be completely healed in six weeks," Rea stated, still not looking up.

"Thanks, babe. Any chance of a lift back to the manor?"

Yep, that got her attention.

Her head snapped up.

"Why can't you call one of the others to get you?"

Pulling my phone out of my pocket, I showed it to her.

"My phone got smashed when I hit the ground."

"I'll call Dragon and ask him to come and get you or have him call one of the others to come," she said, pulling her phone out of her pocket and pressing the call button.

"Dragon, hi, it's Rea. I'm good, thanks. Yes, Mila is fine. I'm calling because Milo is in the A&E and needs a lift home. Can any of you come and get him? Really, oh, okay, no. That's fine. I'll see if we can get him a taxi. Umm, okay, but I'll have to pick Mila up first. Okay. Yeah, see you later," Rea said.

She seemed to be getting more flustered by the second.

My brother had come through, it seemed. I waited for her to finish the call and looked at her with my eyebrows raised.

She was chewing nervously on her lip as she contemplated her phone. Then finally, she looked up.

"Umm, it seems they're all away from the village or busy with other things. I can get you a taxi, or if you are happy to wait half an hour until I finish my shift, I can take you home, but we'll have to get Mila from nursery first."

I wanted to grin so badly. I loved my brothers. Holding my grin back, I replied, "Thanks Rea, I'll take the lift. There's no rush. I have another twenty minutes on the ice, anyway."

"Okay, I'll come back and get you as soon as I'm done," she said before backing out of the cubicle.

Once she was out of sight, I let the grin I had been holding escape. I planned on making this woman mine again, and I knew Dragon had just given me an in. I was going to make myself as indispensable as I could to her. Plus, I couldn't wait to meet her daughter.

CHAPTER 2

REA

I couldn't help but feel like I had somehow been manoeuvred into giving Milo a lift home. I wasn't sure how I'd been manoeuvred, but I knew I had been.

Somehow, I finished the rest of my shift. After handing over the last patient, I let Rosie, the nurse in charge, know I would be back to collect Milo from cubicle four. This got raised eyebrows. While I wasn't unfriendly to the other staff members, I also wasn't the most sociable, so they didn't really know me.

"He's a childhood friend," I muttered to her.

"I didn't say anything," she said.

"No, but I can see you're thinking about it," I replied.

"I think you protest too much," she said, laughing.

Giving her the middle finger, I walked out to the sounds of her laughter and went to the staff room to get changed out of my scrubs.

Grabbing my leather backpack, I threw it over my shoulder and went back to the A&E ward to pick up the man who, even after all he had done, still took up too much time in my mind and my heart.

I got there just as he was fitted with a walking boot. As I stood to the side waiting, I took my time to study him. I had wanted to do this since the night I had glimpsed him in the club we'd been at. I think I knew if I took the time to really look at him, I would find it hard to keep my distance. Even after all he had done to hurt me, my heart still loved him, and I missed him being in my life.

My ex-husband had been right when he asked for a divorce. He'd told me he was tired of competing against the ghost of another man, even if that man was still alive.

I had tried through the two years of our marriage to make it work and forget about Milo. My husband had been a good man, just not the right man for me. He was living his life happily now, married to a wonderful woman with a growing family, and I was happy for them.

If only my heart would sync with my head so I could move on from the man sitting on the hospital bed. He was still the most gorgeous, charismatic man I had ever met. With his black hair, stubbled cheeks and dark eyes fringed with the darkest lashes. He'd always been quiet, content to let his brother and cousins be in the limelight. And I had loved him for ten years before he'd killed that love. I had thought we would always be together. I'm not sure I would ever forgive him for what he did to us. With that thought in mind, I hardened my heart as much as possible and entered the cubicle.

"All done?" I enquired coolly.

The nurse who had been strapping the boot on nodded.

"Yep, he's good to go, Dr Lawson. Here are his discharge papers. I've gone through everything with him, and he knows what painkillers to take if needed."

"Thanks, Lara," I said, taking the papers from her.

Turning to Milo, I muttered, "Come on then, I need to go pick up Mila before I drop you home."

He hopped off the bed and stood to get his balance before taking a step towards me.

"Lead the way, Sugar."

"It's Rea or Dr Lawson. How many times do I have to tell you?" I glowered angrily at him.

He sighed and rubbed his hand across his eyes tiredly.

"Sorry, Rea, I will try to remember."

I huffed slightly and turned to walk out of the room to the front of the A&E building. Then, stopping by a bench, I turned to him and said, "Wait here. I'm going to go and get the car from the staff parking lot."

I waited for him to take a seat. His words stopped me just as I was about to leave.

"Are you really coming back to pick me up, or will you leave me here?"

Looking him dead in the eye, I replied, "Unlike you, Milo, I don't lie. I promised Dragon I would bring you home, and I will. I'll be back in ten minutes."

He grimaced at my words, but I told myself I needed to stay strong.

"Okay," he said, nodding. "I'll be here waiting."

Turning, I hustled to pick up my car to get this ordeal over and done with as quickly as possible. It was already 5:30 p.m., and I needed to pick Mila up by 6 p.m.

Twenty minutes later, I was heading in to pick up the light of my life from the nursery. I left the bane of my existence sitting in my Ford, Maverick. He hadn't said a word since I had pulled up in front of the bench he'd been sitting on. He'd got in and only nodded when I had stopped in front of the nursery and told him I would be ten minutes.

Taking my giggling daughter from the staff member, I covered her face with kisses. Grabbing her bag, I turned to leave when the manager came in from outside and saw me.

"Hi, Dr Lawson. How are you?"

"I'm good, thanks and you?"

"Fantastic. Happy it's Friday. Is that Mila's father in your car? I can't believe how much she looks like him. Where has he been, and do we need to update the records to show he can pick her up?"

Not correcting her assumption, I replied, "Umm, he's in the military, and no, we don't need to update her records, as he won't be here for long."

She looked surprised at my response, but didn't say anything else as I pushed out the door. Opening the passenger door behind him, I strapped my daughter into her car seat and smiled as I listened to her happy babble. I looked up and caught Milo watching us in the wing mirror. Not saying anything, I handed her a snuggie, kissed her head and closed her door. I knew she would be asleep before we hit the high street, and it was another twenty minutes from there to the manor house.

Milo was silent all the way to the manor. It was getting on for 6:30 p.m. when I pulled into the family parking at the back of the manor. I recognised Milo's mum, Maggie, but didn't know the woman she was talking to or the two blonde girls with them. They looked like they had just come from school and were still in uniforms. Hearing bikes behind me, I watched as four motorcycles pulled around me and parked. Coming to a stop behind the vehicle that the woman and children were standing at. I checked on Mila in the mirror and saw she was still sleeping.

Feeling a light touch on my arm, I turned to Milo, who looked troubled.

"Thanks for dropping me off, Rea. I'm sorry for making this so hard on you. I can see that spending time in my company hurts you, which wasn't my intention. But know if you need my brothers or me, you just have to call. Okay."

Swallowing the lump in my throat, I nodded.

"Okay."

"Do you have all our numbers?" he queried.

"Yes. Dray put them all in my phone."

He nodded.

"That's good. I'll let you go and get your sleeping beauty home. Thanks again for the lift."

With that, he got out of the car and hobbled his way towards the group that was congregating, questions being fired at him. Reaper had been one of the riders, and I could see he was furious with Milo about something.

I watched for a little longer before putting my car in gear and reversing to turn around. I was just about to pull away when something had me look up. Maggie, Milo's mum, was standing watching me. She smiled and waved. I couldn't help but return her smile and wave. She had always been good to me when Milo and I were together.

Leaving them, I couldn't help but feel sad. When Milo and I split up, not only had I lost him and our baby, but I had also lost his siblings, cousins and his mum and dad.

Straightening my shoulders, I decided that even if Milo and I didn't make it, there was no reason for me not to see the rest of his family.

Tomorrow, Mila and I would go to the Trickster Café for lunch.

CHAPTER 3

ONYX

It had been over a month since the lift I had gotten home from Rea. I kept coming back to the confusion I had seen on her face when I backed off, not pushing to see her again.

I'd had second thoughts about pursuing her again when I'd watched her come out of the nursery with her little girl, and they had both been laughing. The love that shone from Rea's face as she talked to her daughter had been beautiful to watch. The punch in the gut I had got when I caught my first real look at her little girl had knocked the breath out of me. She had the same colouring as me, but the rest of her was all Rea, from the shape of her face to her nose. She was beautiful and so happy.

I watched as Rea buckled her in, talking to her all the time, and how Mila responded in baby babble. I knew there was no way I would have the shit storm we were in with the ACES touch these two.

So, I'd backed away from trying to start anything with her again.

I knew from the others that she had been to the café several times and met up with both Noni and Avy for coffee. Dragon still saw her, and I knew the brotherhood was confused that I wasn't all up in her business. I'd been reamed out good and hard by Reaper after my accident. I'd taken it because he wasn't wrong. I shouldn't have been out by myself.

We'd spent the last month beating back the ACES and their attempts at sabotage. So far, we'd replaced the windows in the café twice after bricks had been thrown through the windows. They'd attempted a break-in at the bakery and the garage, but we'd installed loud as fuck alarms and had caught them on camera. The ones that had attempted the break-ins were now guests of her majesty's pleasure.

They'd tried to get into the pub, but Liam's guys were good, and they'd quickly removed them from the premises. Then it was selling drugs in our pub car park, which had pissed off two of our prospects who'd beat the shit out of the ones they'd caught and tied them up to wait for the cops to come.

All the crap floating around the club was why I'd backed off from Rea. She didn't need any of this touching her, not with a child to protect.

So far, it had been petty stuff, annoying, but nothing that we couldn't handle. But I knew it wouldn't last. Blood would be spilt soon, and I only hoped it wasn't ours.

I was right, blood was spilt, but it wasn't ours or theirs. The blood ACES spilt started a war.

We'd just finished church and were standing around the bar in the clubhouse, chatting and having a beer. There was talk about making a trip to the beach that weekend as the weather looked good and no rain was forecast when my phone rang.

Pulling it out of my pocket, my brows creased into a frown when I read the name on the front. The room was silenced as I answered the call.

"Rea, what's wrong?"

I heard her breath hitch slightly, and I could tell she had been crying. In the background, I could hear Mila screaming.

"Milo," she whispered. "I need you to come to the hospital. Bring your brothers. I only want to go through what's happened once."

"Baby, are you okay?" I asked softly.

She whimpered slightly, and I could hear someone asking a question about pain.

"No. Can you get here quickly? They'll let you back. Just tell them your name. I've asked my colleagues to look out for you," she replied before ending the call.

I looked up at my brothers. My heart was pounding fast and hard in my chest like a drum.

Something was very wrong with Rea.

"Onyx, what do you need?" Reaper asked.

"We need to get to the hospital. Rea's hurt. She asked that I bring my brothers because she only wants to go through it once," I said, already moving to the clubhouse doors.

Reaper nodded and looked around the clubhouse.

"Dragon, Draco, Rogue and I are coming. Hawk, you, Navy and Bull are in charge. Check on the prospects at the gate and lock things down until we know what is happening. Once we have more news, I'll call you from the hospital. Dragon drive Onyx in the Land Rover, the rest of you on bikes."

I ran out of the clubhouse to the parking lot at the house and was in the passenger seat before Dragon reached his door. I was so anxious, my hands were clenched, my knee bouncing, I couldn't keep my legs still.

Rea hadn't sounded good.

We lit out of the property, going faster than the speed limit, but it still seemed like the half-hour drive was taken at a snail's pace.

Dragon dropped me at the main doors, and I ran in as he went to find a parking spot.

I didn't have to wait long as the nurse at the front desk recognised me and motioned for me to come to the back.

I stopped in front of her and said, "My brothers will be here just now. They're parking, but Rea asked me to bring them."

She nodded before replying, "Okay, I'll let the front desk know, but first, we need you to get your daughter to calm down. She hasn't stopped crying since they came in, and it's not doing Rea any good, as she can't hold her right now. We have them in a private room in A&E. I must warn you that Rea looks worse than it is, other than her arm, which is broken. The rest is just bruising."

We'd been walking while she talked and had stopped by a door at the end of the corridor. I could hear Mila screaming through the thick door and Rea murmuring softly.

I took a deep breath to calm down before nodding to the nurse to open the door.

My breath stopped when I got my first look at Rea lying in bed. Her face was unrecognisable from all the bruising and abrasions. She had stitches through her left eyebrow, and her eye was completely swollen and closed. Her nose looked like it had been broken. It had a white strap across the bridge. More worrying was her arm, which was clearly broken by the looks of the swelling and how she was cradling it, but nothing had been done about it yet. I wondered why when the nurse who was holding the screaming Mila turned as the door opened, letting us in.

"Finally, you're here. Take your daughter so we can get Rea sorted out. She wouldn't let us sort out her arm until you got here because she didn't want to leave her daughter. So here you go, Daddy," she said as she thrust a screaming Mila into my arms.

Shocked, my arms closed around the screaming child, and I held her firmly to my chest, murmuring softly to her.

"Shh, princess, shh. I'm here now." I pressed a kiss to the thick black curls on her head.

She stopped crying as soon as she was in my arms. Her eyes closed as she let out little whimpers and immediately fell asleep against my chest. I hadn't even made it into the room.

Walking over to the bed with my precious bundle held firmly to my chest, I bent and pressed my lips to Rea's head. Her hand grasped my hand where it rested on the bed. I murmured into her hair, "Sugar, I'm here. Let the nurses sort you out so we can find out what happened. I have Mila."

She lifted her head and looked at me as best as she could, considering the bruising swelling around her eyes.

"Only you are to hold her, nobody else. Don't let her out of your sight," she said adamantly.

"I promise I won't let her out of my sight, sweetheart. Dragon and the rest are here. They are just waiting to be brought back."

"Rea, we really need to get that arm sorted. Your man can stay here with Mila while we head to x-ray. You'll be back soon," the nurse who had brought me in said from the door, where she was standing with a wheelchair. I could see my brothers behind her, their faces tight with anger as they took in the damage done to Rea.

"Okay," Rea whimpered as she sat up and swung her legs to the side.

Her gown opened slightly with her back to me, and I could see the extent of her bruising across her back and what looked like a boot print on her kidneys.

I must have made a noise because Mila shifted restlessly, and Rea looked back at me.

"Keep her safe for me," she said as the nurse helped her stand and shuffled slowly to the door.

"I promise she won't leave my sight. I'll keep her safe. Go get x-rayed so we can get you sorted and home."

The nurse had her in the chair and whisked her down the corridor to x-ray. I tilted my head to Dragon, and he nodded before following them. It wasn't just Mila who we needed to keep safe.

"You keeping it together, brother?" Reaper asked, his face showing his concern for me.

I nodded, taking a careful seat and settled Mila against my chest, cupping her little butt in one hand and the other rubbing gently up and down her back. I looked down at the beautiful little girl in my arms, her face still showing tears, her little lips pursed as she slept.

I looked up at my brothers as they leaned against the wall on the far side of the room.

"For now," I replied. "Depending on what Rea says, I may need some time in the ring if it's bad. Let's wait and see."

Turning my attention to Draco, I said, "Can you call mum and fill her in? Have her set up the room attached to mine for Mila. I know we have cribs and stuff in the attic from when they did emergency fostering."

"Will do," he said, taking his phone out of his pocket and leaving the room.

That left only me, Rogue, and Reaper in the room. I relaxed slightly, but knew I wouldn't fully relax until I got them home.

"Rogue, can you have Avy and Noni head to Rea's place and pick up clothing for Rea and Mila. Make sure the fridge is cleaned out and have them bring it all back to the manor?"

He nodded and got on his phone with his sister. I sighed and leaned my head tiredly back against the chair, trying to get the image of Rea's face out of my head.

'Fuck, they had really worked her over.'

"You stepping up, Onyx?" Reaper asked quietly.

Opening my eyes, I looked at the man resting against the wall next to me, seeing not only my president but the man that had been at my back since the day I was born. It would be an achievement if I could be half the man he was.

"Yeah, I stayed away for the last month, not wanting to pull them into the shit we have swirling around us with the ACES. Now I'm wondering if it hasn't affected them, anyway."

"If it's them, they'll be dealt with," Reaper assured me.

"I know," I agreed, just as we heard Rea and Dragon talking to the nurse outside the door.

The first thing Rea did as they pushed her into the room was check on Mila. Her face relaxed as soon as she saw her still asleep on my chest.

The nurse helped her back onto the bed and tucked the blanket around her before handing her a cup of water and some tablets.

She said brusquely, "Take these. It will help with the pain. They'll come and get you shortly to set your arm."

Rea nodded, taking the pills, settling back in bed, and closing her eyes.

"Rea hun, I know you're tired, but can you tell us what happened?"

She opened one good eye and tried to push herself up on the bed with her one good arm, her other arm held immobile in a sling. Rea groaned in pain. Dragon rushed over and helped her, making me grumble. He grinned at me as he patted her pillows and made sure she was comfortable.

"Thanks, Dragon," she smiled slightly at him before turning to us and saying, "I had just picked Mila up from the nursery and was walking to the back car park because there is a burst water line in the front of the building. I had just strapped her in when they came out of nowhere. They grabbed me and pushed me up against the vehicle. Of course, I fought back. I haven't forgotten any of what you taught me, but there were three of them. I managed to get one of them good in the balls by twisting them, and another had a pretty good scratch across his eyes when I went for them. But when they got me down on the ground, they proceeded to clobber the daylights out of me. As you can see," she said, pointing at her face.

"They only stopped when another car pulled in and shouted at them. They threatened Mila and gave me a message for you."

She tilted her head slightly towards me.

"Tell the Crows that the ACES say this is only the beginning. It will get worse if they carry on their vendetta."

There was a round of *'Fucks'* from around the room.

"What I don't understand is why you? I've kept my distance for just this reason because I didn't want that filth to touch you," I asked.

"Making decisions for me again without talking to me, Milo," she hissed angrily at me.

I winced slightly because she wasn't wrong. That was exactly what I'd done.

Turning away from me, she looked at Reaper before continuing. "From what I could gather from the words they threw at me while they were laying into me, they assumed Milo was Mila's father, and we were separated after they saw me drop him off at the manor a month ago. They couldn't touch the rest of the women because they always have someone with them, but I was an easy target."

I let out an agonised groan at her words. It was my fault. I should have made sure she was covered. Why didn't I think of them watching us?

"Onyx, don't take this one on, brother. We should have thought about it, between Dragon visiting and Rea socialising at the café. It's on all of us, not just you," Reaper stated.

"Are you able to describe any of them, Rea?" Draco questioned.

She nodded her head. "Yeah, give me my backpack. I wrote them down as soon as I could so I wouldn't forget."

'Jesus,' I thought to myself. 'She was strong. To think of doing that while in pain.'

Rea rifled through her back, searching, and then pulled out a notebook. Opening it up, she flipped through until she found a page and tore it out.

"Here," she said, handing the page to Reaper.

"Just so you know, the police think it's a mugging. Wrong place, wrong time thing. I didn't say anything about the message. I also only gave them a vague description of the guys who attacked me. I know you guys will want to sort this yourself."

This got her a grin from all the men in the room.

"You're fucking awesome, babe," Rogue said, a broad grin on his face.

Sitting in the chair next to her bed, I gripped her hand tight where it lay on the bed next to me, happy that she had let me. The strength in this woman.

She just shrugged. "Only one name, though. They didn't really speak to each other, but as they ran, one shouted to the other one and used his name. He shouted Chad."

Reaper straightened from the wall. "Chad? Skinny, with dreadlocks, and could use a bath?"

Rea nodded, "Yeah, that's right. Do you know him?"

"He's the one that started shit in the café when they tried to initiate Ben. What's the bet that the other two with him are the same twatwaffles that came into the café that day. I'll speak to the lads and see what information they have on the three. Don't worry, babe, we'll get this sorted," Reaper assured her.

There was a knock on the door. They had come to collect Rea to get her arm set. Dragon followed again while we waited some more. I could see that the others were itching to find out if it was the same three.

"Reap, why don't you, Draco, and Rogue head out and find out if it was them? Dragon can stay here with Rea and me as he's the one who drove me here," I said.

"Are you sure?" he questioned.

"Yeah, as soon as Rea's released, I'm taking them straight to the manor. I don't care if she's not happy about it. She's going to need help with Mila with her broken arm. So the sooner you get these shits, the better. The only thing I ask is when you find them, I get a piece."

"Of course, brother," Draco assured, walking over to fist-bump me. Then, he bent and pressed a gentle kiss to the top of Mila's head. Rogue and Reaper followed suit before they all left.

While we waited, I phoned mum to have her send one of the prospects over with a car seat for Mila. An hour later, we were able to leave the hospital after only a small argument with Rea about coming home with us. It was only after Dragon pointed out that she would need help with Mila, as she only had one arm and her neighbour Rose was away for the next three months, that she caved.

Mila was just stirring as we pulled up into the family parking behind the manor. I handed her to my mum, who was waiting for us, along with her diaper bag that I knew had her bottle in. Leaving her in my mother's capable hands, I turned to the woman who still held my heart. The painkillers they had given her had kicked in about twenty minutes ago, and she was fast asleep. Sliding my hands behind her back and under her legs, I picked her up as gently as I could and carried her through the house and up the stairs to my room. Settling her in my bed, I thought about how right she looked lying there and vowed I would fix everything I broke.

I had six weeks to do it.

Rea was signed off work until her arm was healed, and I aimed to do all I could to get her to love me again.

Leaving her sleeping peacefully, I headed downstairs to the rest of the family, knowing they would have lots of questions that needed answering.

CHAPTER 4

REA

The pain in my ribs woke me up. Squinting with my one good eye, I looked around the unfamiliar room, wondering where I was.

I jumped slightly when a voice asked from next to me, "Sugar, what do you need? Are you in pain?"

Relaxing slightly when I recognised Milo's voice, I turned my head toward him, moaning a little at the stiffness in my neck.

His bedside lamp clicked on, and I shaded my eyes with my good hand.

"Sorry, sweetheart," he whispered, dimming the light slightly. "Do you need another pain pill?"

"Please, but first, I need to use the bathroom," I said, hissing slightly as I tried to sit up.

"Baby, stop moving. Give me a moment, and I'll help you up," Milo said, getting up and moving to my side of the bed.

He was dressed in only a pair of trackie bottoms, his chest bare. He had changed a lot since I last saw him without clothes on. He was broader and more muscular than he used to be. I hated to admit it, but he looked delicious.

'Typical,' I grumbled softly to myself. *'He looked fantastic, and I looked like a pile of dog poo.'*

I heard him chuckle softly as he came to a stop next to the bed.

"You don't look like dog poo, Sugar. You are still as beautiful today as you were when I first saw you. In fact, I think you're more gorgeous now than you were then."

"Smooth talker," I said, smiling slightly. "Help me up."

"First pain pills, then I'll get you to the bathroom," he said, handing me a couple of pills before opening a bottle of water and handing me that.

Taking it all, I drank down the pills and guzzled the water, only then realising how thirsty I was. Finishing the bottle of water, I hand it back to him.

"I'll grab you another one when we get back from the bathroom," he told me as he slipped his hands under me and lifted me up. My entire body protested, and a little whimper escaped my clenched lips.

"I'm sorry, sweetheart. The pain pills should kick in soon. I should have woken you up when you were due the last lot, but you were sleeping so soundly I thought it best not to."

"It's okay," I said softly, laying my head on his chest.

Sleeping was better for me in the long run.

He set me on the floor in the bathroom before turning on the light. I blinked my eyes as the light shone brightly.

"Do you need me to help you, or can you manage," he asked as he gently tilted my head up to him.

"I can manage, but don't go too far, just in case."

"I won't. I'll be right outside," Onyx assured me. "Just shout if you need me."

Looking down, I noticed that someone must have undressed me as I was no longer wearing the scrubs they sent me home in. Instead, I was in a pair of panties and a t-shirt that hung to mid-thigh.

Finishing up, I washed the one hand that was not in a sling. Lifting my head to look in the mirror. I sighed when I saw the damage that was done to my face. No wonder my head felt like it was going to explode. At least the only things broken was my nose and my arm. The way they were laying into me, I thought it would be worse.

There was a knock on the door, and Milo pushed it open slightly, asking through the crack, "Babe, are you okay?"

"Yeah," I answered him, slowly shuffling towards the door. "I'm done."

He pushed the door open just as I got there, picking me up. He took me back to bed, laying me down gently before adjusting a pillow under my broken arm for support.

"What's the time," I asked him.

He walked back around to his side of the bed and grabbed his phone to check.

"Just gone 3 a.m. I've just checked on Mila, and she is still fast asleep."

"Where did you put her?" I asked curiously.

He pointed to a door that was standing ajar next to where the wardrobes were.

"She's in there. I had them bring in a crib and set it up for her. I knew you would want her close by."

"Thank you," I whispered gratefully. My eyes grew heavy with sleep as the painkillers kicked in.

"No thanks needed, Sugar," he whispered softly, pressing a soft kiss to the corner of my mouth before settling next to me in bed.

I didn't even try to protest because the truth was I'd missed him, and him sleeping next to me made me feel safe.

The next time I woke up, I was alone in bed, and the sun shone through the gap in the curtains. I turned my head towards the room Mila had been in and saw the door was open. I guessed that Milo had gotten up with her. I was surprised at how little it concerned me that he had taken over her care. Maybe it was because I knew deep down that he was still the same person he'd always been.

Slowly I sat up, groaning as pain shot through my entire body. I managed to make it to the edge of the bed and was sitting there wondering how I was going to get up when there was a knock on the door. Abby peered around the edge.

We'd met on one of my visits to the café, and I could see why Kane had not let her slip away. She was a straight-talking-take-no-nonsense type of woman with a great sense of humour. I was sure it helped that she was gorgeous. Although, according to her, her arse was way too big. Kane didn't seem to agree and was quite often seen with his hand on said arse.

"Hey, Rea, I thought I heard you stirring through the baby monitor. Do you need a hand getting up?"

"Please, Abs. I need to take some painkillers, and I'm desperate for a shower," I replied.

"Painkillers should be on your bedside table with some water," she said, coming into the room to pick up the box of painkillers. Taking two out, she handed them to me and then gave me a glass of water.

"Mila is downstairs having a ball with my girls and Maggie. Onyx is out doing something with the rest of the men, but he asked me to let you know he would be back by this afternoon. He wanted me to tell you to take it easy today. We'll all look after Mila for you, so don't worry about that. Nothing like a cute baby to make us all broody," she said with a little grin.

"Let me help you to the bathroom, and then I'll go find something to wrap around your arm to keep it dry. Then we'll get you in the shower. Onyx had us pack you a bag with clothing. I'll find you something to wear while you're showering. Once you're done, I will see if one of the prospects can help you down the stairs to the couch in the sitting room. That way, you can still be part of what is happening in the house and spend some time with Mila."

She rambled on while helping me stand up. We then proceeded in a slow shuffle to the bathroom.

"I'll just be a minute, and then I'll be back. If you're unsteady, make sure you sit down," Abby instructed before closing the bathroom door on her way out, making me smile a little. I could see why she made a good first lady. Bossiness came naturally to her.

I'd just finished brushing my teeth when she returned and knocked on the door.

"Come in," I said.

"Hope you're good with me helping you, hun, because there is no way we can do this without you getting naked, so hope you're not shy."

Abby grinned at me, her eyes sparkling with laughter.

I snorted slightly, "Honestly, I don't care. I just want to be clean again. So, if it doesn't bother you, it certainly won't bother me."

"Good, let's get you in the shower then," she said briskly.

We got me undressed and wrapped me in a towel. Abby made sounds of sympathy when she saw the mess my body was in.

"Shit, babe, that must hurt like hell. I hope the guys find the scum who did this and put some hurt on them," Abby muttered while wrapping my arm.

She had stripped down with me but was in a swimming costume.

"To keep it from being weird," she smiled at me.

This made me chuckle, which in turn made me groan as pain stabbed through me.

"Stop making me laugh," I muttered. "It hurts."

"Sorry," she said with a small grin helping me into the shower. "Let me wash your hair, and then I'll leave you to handle the rest," she told me, helping me sit on the plastic chair she had put in the shower.

Tilting my head back, I moaned in relief at the hot water hitting my aching body. Abby made quick work of washing and conditioning my hair before helping me stand, handing me a loofah with shower gel when she got out of the shower.

"Thanks, Abby. I'm sure this isn't something you ever thought you'd have to do."

She shrugged as she grabbed a towel and wrapped it around herself.

"It needed to be done. That's what families do for each other. Rea, we help when needed. I'm going to get out of this costume and change. I'll bring your clothes and put them on the sink for you. You just have to shout if you need a hand getting dressed or help to take the plastic off your cast. I'll wait for you in the bedroom."

Removing the towel we'd wrapped me in for a bit of modesty, I threw the soggy mess in the corner of the shower and washed yesterday off me. Getting out of the shower, I noticed I was moving a little easier with the combination of hot water and painkillers.

I managed to get my knickers and trackie bottoms on but couldn't get the t-shirt on. Holding it to my chest, I shuffled out of the bathroom and into the bedroom. Abby was sitting on the neatly made bed, waiting for me.

"I can't get the t-shirt on. Is there a button-up in my bag," I asked Abby.

She shook her head and got up to go towards the wardrobes.

"No, only t-shirts. Let me grab you one of Onyx's shirts. I'm sure he must have a flannel in here somewhere," she said, rifling through the cupboard.

"Aha," she said, holding up a dark green flannel and bringing it over to me to help me into it.

It swamped me but was nice and soft against my skin. I wouldn't be able to wear a bra for a while, so this was a better solution as it gave me more coverage than a t-shirt would.

"Sit here for a minute while I go and check to see which prospects are around," Abby said, helping me sit down on the bed.

I was exhausted. Between the shower and getting dressed, I could have gone back to sleep, but I needed something to eat. It was only then that I realised my hair was still up in a towel.

I groaned because there was no way I would be able to brush it as I couldn't lift my arms. My eyes welled with tears as I realised how much I would have to rely on everyone for help.

Just then, Abby came back in with a good-looking, well-built clean-cut guy, probably in his mid-twenties, with blond hair and blue eyes.

"Oh honey, what's wrong?" Abby asked, rushing over when she saw the tears on my face.

"I can't brush my hair," I whispered pathetically. "It just hit me how much I'm going to rely on all of you to do stuff for me. I'm not used to it. I've been by myself for a long time."

Abby smiled at me before saying kindly, "Ah, hun, don't worry, you'll be up and around in no time. In the meantime, enjoy being pampered. Now, let's grab your brush and have Bond carry you downstairs. I'll have my Bren sort your hair for you, so don't worry on that count. Then we'll get you some breakfast, and you can snuggle with your little one. Pretty soon, you'll be feeling much better. Let me introduce you to your ride downstairs today. Rea meet Bond."

"Pleased to meet you, Rea, and it's not a hardship to carry a beautiful woman around," he winked cheekily at me.

I snorted a laugh at him before replying, "Thanks, Bond. Although I don't think I'm beautiful at the moment, but it's kind of you to say so."

He shrugged at my comment and said, "Eh, you say tamato, I say tomato. It's all in the eye of the beholder. Now I know there's another beautiful young lady downstairs who would like to see her mum, so how about we get you down there?"

Picking me up gently, he carried me down the stairs carefully with barely a jolt and deposited me on the couch in what I knew was the family room from my visits over the years as a teenager. Not much had changed in it.

Then Maggie was there with Mila and Abby's two girls, Bren and Ellie. After giving Mila some love, Maggie put her on a blanket on the floor with a few toys and Ellie to keep her entertained.

Abby brought me tea and toast for breakfast. Then, she and Maggie sat down with cups of tea to keep me company while I ate.

"Bren, Rea needs her hair brushed and plaiting. Do you think you could do that for her when she's had breakfast," Abby asked.

Bren was more than happy to brush my hair and plait it for me. While she was doing this, I fell asleep, not feeling the kiss on my forehead and the whispered words from Maggie as she covered me.

"It's good to have you back home with us where you belong, sweet girl. Maybe now my boy will find happiness again."

CHAPTER 5

MILO

I'd not wanted to leave Rea to wake up alone, but Reaper had called to say that they had the three dickheads that had put their hands on her and to come down to the abattoir.

I'd taken the baby monitor down and left it with my mum so that she could get Mila when she woke. Then I made my way through the cold dawn, the sun just rising in the sky, burning through the early morning mist.

It took about ten minutes to walk to the abattoir. From the front, it looked derelict, and we kept it like that for a reason. We'd added signs warning of structural damage and no entry signs.

I entered the abattoir through the path we had cut through the woods by the cottages and around the back of the building that couldn't be seen from the road. This part of the building was well-kept, and we'd added water and electricity. Our weapons were housed in an underground bunker under the abattoir. Due to the nature of what it had been used for, it had convenient drainage facilities for the type of things we may have to do to send a warning.

All my brothers and two of the prospects were waiting for me. The only ones missing were the prospects Skinny and Blaze and the originals, Thor, Dog, and Gunny. I knew the prospects were at the gate watching the security feeds, and I assumed the originals were on the women and businesses we ran.

They all looked up as I entered.

"Where are they?" I demanded, scanning the room and taking note of the table set up in the corner with tools for extracting information.

"We have them in separate holding rooms. I wanted to discuss how this was going to go," Reaper said.

"What do you mean, discuss it? We get what information we can and kill the fuckers," I said angrily.

"Definitely that," Reaper agreed. "But I also want to send a little message to the big man."

"Okay," I said, slightly mollified. "As long as I still get to hurt them."

Reaper grinned at me, "Of course, brother. No question about it. Rea has always been one of ours. They'll hurt. At the moment, we have them gagged and fitted with hoods. You can have dreadlocks and one of the others, but I need one to be able to speak. Doesn't mean we can't hurt him a little, but I need him to be able to deliver a message."

I looked around at the rest of the brothers and noticed Bond was bouncing on his toes.

"You okay, Bond?"

"Please can I have a go at one of the fuckers," he said a little maniacally, his hands in a praying gesture. "I had to watch you carry the Doc upstairs last night. You all know my background, and I need to make them hurt a little. I know I'm just a prospect, but fuck, she's half their size."

The rest chuckled a little at him, but I could see it had really bothered him seeing Rea hurt.

I walked over to the table and picked up one of the disposable coveralls and boot covers before nodding to him and saying, "Bring one of them out to the table. Leave the hood on when you bring him out. Then come over here and get suited up."

Bond's face lit up in glee as he hurried to the first door and opened it. He came out soon after dragging the first one out by his dreadlocks. He was whimpering and thrashing around as he was being dragged along the floor. Bond picked him up and threw him in the chair, then proceeded to duct tape his ankles to the chair.

When Bond pulled the hood off his head, I was surprised at how young he was. He couldn't have been more than twenty-one.

"Young one, huh," I said, looking at my brothers as they leaned against the wall.

"Old enough to beat on a defenceless woman, threaten a baby, our sister and threaten to rape our Pres' woman. So old enough to face the consequences," Draco replied in a hard tone. I looked at dreadlocks. His eyes were wild as they searched around the room for an escape. He sagged against the back of the chair when he realised there was no way out except through the wall of men standing around the room.

Reaper went to the instrument table and selected a knife. He then approached Dreadlock and crouched in front of him.

He ran the knife along the top of Dreadlock's thigh. Cutting through the denim, his blood flowed to the top.

"Did I not warn you what would happen if you continued to piss us off with your drug dealing in our town?" Reaper asked conversationally before making another cut down the other thigh.

Dreadlocks screamed behind his gag. I sniggered a little.

"Pres, if you want him to answer, you may have to remove the gag, just saying. Me? I'm happy for you to continue cutting him, so if that's what you need to do, go right ahead," I said with a slight smirk.

Reaper grinned up at me, his eyes dark with anger.

"Huh? Brother, you might be right. I probably should take the gag off. Silly me," he said, sliding his knife under the gag and digging it into Dreadlock's cheek, cutting it deeply before cutting the gag off.

"Now, where was I? Just one more brother before you and Bond take over," Reaper assured me as he slid the knife up Dreadlock's neck to his ear where he had a gauge, sliding the knife in the hole of the gauge he pulled down sharply ripping it out of Dreadlocks ear.

The screaming was music to my ears. We spent the next couple of hours extracting as much information as possible from two of them.

And it was a lot.

Rogue made notes on a map of different drug-holding sites and their routes. There was more around our village than we liked, but we would take care of them once we had finished here. The third man we left alone, but we had him listen to everything we did to his two companions. Reaper did what he did best. He frightened the shit out of him by whispering to him, telling him what we were doing and how it would be his turn once we were done.

Nothing like a bit of psychological warfare to terrify a man. He was shaking and crying by the time we were done with his mates. I knew he would have been pleading just like they had if he wasn't gagged.

Once we had all we could get out of the two of them that were now hanging on the meat hooks that Dragon had stuck through their shoulders. We'd had to wake them a couple of times after they passed out, but I didn't think we would get much more out of them this time as there was no response when we tried to wake them.

Bull walked over and checked their pulse before shaking his head and walking away.

"Onyx and Bond, you two get changed and burn those coveralls in the barrel we started outside. Cairo and I'll deal with the bodies. We'll drop the remains in the pig pens next door tonight," Draco said, suiting up and throwing an coverall at Cairo.

It was nearly dark when I walked out. We'd been at this the whole day. I walked over to the fire and disposed of the bloody coveralls and boot covers. Once that was done, I went to the trough and walked through the bleach bath that had been set up to rid the bottom of my boots of any remaining blood, not that I was expecting there to be any, as my boot covers had remained intact, but we were nothing if not careful.

Seeing a cooler bag on the picnic table under the trees, I opened it up, grabbed a bottle of water and downed it before taking a seat to wait for the others to finish up. Bond wasn't far behind me. I nodded when he walked up and got his own bottle of water.

"You good?" I asked him.

"I'm good," he assured me.

Looking at him, I saw he was fine with what we had done.

I nodded and left him to his thoughts. He'd gone up to the house earlier after Reaper got a call from Abby to help bring Rea down to the family room, and when he came back, he'd really upped his game. I guess seeing her in the cold light of day had affected him. The rest slowly made their way outside, each taking a turn to drop their coverall in the burning barrel and walking through the bleach bath before making their way over to us.

The only ones missing were Draco and Cairo. They'd be a little while still. I knew Draco would want to make sure the prospect knew what he was doing.

"What are we doing with the last one?" Dragon questioned.

Reaper was silent for a moment. He looked like he was gathering his thoughts before he spoke.

"I want him delivered right to the front door of the arsehole in London. But before we do, Rogue, can you grab the Crow branding iron from Church at the clubhouse? We have a fire going, and it seems a shame to waste it."

Rogue nodded and took off for the clubhouse. Reaper was seriously pissed off if we were marking our enemy with our brand.

"The fucker needs to get the message that we are done playing. I want this gobshite delivered right to his front door just after we blow the shit out of all the places we marked on the map. I want him to know that we know who he is and can get to him if we want to. I'm sorry, Onyx. I know you wanted to spend time with Rea, but I think we need to hit back hard, and it needs to be done tonight. I'm tired of playing with this fucker. He thinks he gets to play God because he is in the government. Once we clear out this lot of drugs, I think we need to sit down with Gunny's woman and see if we can get some good blackmail material on this guy. We need to try and get rid of him once and for all," Reaper continued as we waited for Rogue to come back.

It wasn't long before Rogue returned with the branding iron. He handed it to Reaper. It was made of thick steel and had a rough depiction of a crow in the centre of a circle. It had been made by my great-grandfather when they originally started the MC. They'd branded their crows onto their shoulders rather than the tattoo we now use.

Reaper walked over to the fire barrel and added the branding iron.

"Bond, go get the little turd, leave the head sack on and gag in his mouth. We don't need the women investigating the screaming," Reaper instructed.

It didn't take Bond long to drag the remaining ACES member out. There was already a stain on the front of his pants where he'd pissed himself. Draco and Cairo, their coveralls covered in blood, came out to watch.

Bond shoved the guy to his knees in front of Reaper.

Reaper tapped him on the side of his face, making the gangbanger turn towards him.

"I have a message I want you to deliver. Nod, if you understand me."

The gangbanger nodded frantically.

"We're going to deliver you to your boss, and I want you to tell him that The Crows are done fucking around. The ACES are to leave our territory. If the ACES don't, he'll not like what happens next. Nod if you understand."

The gangbanger again nodded that he understood.

"Good, we have one more message for you to take to him," Reaper motioned for Hawk and Navy to come closer.

"Grab his arms and hold him tight. Bond, pull his shirt up. I need his stomach," Reaper instructed as he pulled the glowing branding iron from the fire.

The three of them held the gangbanger fast as Reaper pressed the brand to his stomach. When he pulled it away, there was a clear depiction of our brand showing. The gangbanger had been screaming behind his gag the whole time. Snot and tears ran down his face until he'd eventually passed out and was hanging limp in Hawk and Navy's hands.

"Who's doing the drop?" I asked.

"I'll take him," Bond volunteered.

Reaper shook his head. "No, we need you tonight. I'm going to have Blaze and Gunny take him. Dog and Thor can be on security at the gate tonight. I need Gunny to get Beverly afterwards from wherever he's stashed her so we can get something to hold over this wanker. I'm sure she's got something or knows something. While I'm sorting that, the rest of you go to the armoury and load us up for tonight.

"After that's done, clean up and head to the house to grab something to eat. Be ready to leave at 1:00 a.m. That should give Draco and Cairo enough time to dispose of the bodies and get back here."

We all nodded and dispersed, leaving Reaper to call in the Originals and give them their orders.

We loaded up the ammunition and explosives we'd need for tonight before heading to the house for supper. I needed to grab a shower first, so I scooted past the kitchen and headed to my room before anyone saw me. I didn't want to sully my family with what I'd done today.

Once I was done cleaning up, I headed down to the kitchen, which was the hub in this house, to find all the family there. Mila was in a highchair at the kitchen table, being entertained by Reaper's youngest, Ellie. I dropped a kiss on each of their heads before looking for my mother and finding her by the stove, showing Reaper's eldest daughter Bren something.

"Mum," I called out.

She looked up from the stove. Seeing me, my mum knew what I wanted without me having to say anything.

"She's in the family lounge, son. You may want to wake her up. Supper will be on the table in twenty minutes."

Nodding, I turned and headed out of the kitchen to the family lounge, slowing as I noticed the door was only open a crack. Pushing it open, I saw Rea asleep on the couch. Her face was relaxed, although her bruising was worse today than yesterday. I winced a little, looking at them. I'd asked Abby to help her shower before we all left that morning. She'd been in the kitchen getting coffee as I'd walked out. I knew Rea would want to clean up and was a little sad I hadn't been the one to help her. But I was taking it slowly. I had a lot to make up for.

Sitting down on the side of the couch, I ran my hand gently across her uninjured cheek. Her eyelids fluttered, and for a moment, she looked at me with all the love she had felt for me in our past before she realised where she was, and her eyes lowered, shutting me out.

"Hey, Sugar, time to wake up. Supper will be ready soon. Do you need help to get up?"

She nodded at me, wincing slightly as she tried to sit up. Standing, I gently pulled her up next to me. She groaned as she straightened up.

"Fuck," she whimpered. "Everything hurts."

Pulling her gently against me, I had her lean her weight against me until she was steadier on her feet. Then, she wrapped her good arm around me and tucked her head under my chin. We stood like that until she was ready to move. I didn't rush her. It felt so good having her in my arms.

"I need to go to the bathroom before supper," she said, tilting her head slightly to look up at me.

"Do you need me to carry you?" I asked her.

She shook her head. "No, I need to start moving, or I'm going to stiffen up. I also need my next dose of pain pills. Can you ask Abby where she put them?"

"Of course, Babe. Let's get you to the bathroom first and then to the dining room, okay?" I tell her.

We slowly make our way out of the lounge to the downstairs bathroom. I helped her inside and left her to do what she needed to do. Ten minutes later, she was out looking slightly better with clear eyes.

"Better?" I asked.

"Yeah," she replied, putting her arm back around my waist as I took most of her weight. We shuffled down the passage to the dining room.

We heard the voices and laughter before we got to the door. With all the new family and club members, we'd had to open the table up and add all the leaves. We were always missing a few people, though, as we always had two prospects at the gate checking security and keeping an eye on the computers. We'd set up CCTV on all our business, and Avy was usually at the pub, but with what was going down tonight, Reaper had arranged for one of Liam's employees to run the pub tonight.

They all fell silent as we shuffled our way into the room until Mila let out a squeal, *"Mama, mama."*

Looking down, I could see Rea smiling at her daughter as much as she could, and she shuffled closer to her before kissing her on the forehead.

"Hello, baby girl. Have you been having fun?"

This caused her to let out a stream of baby babble, making us all laugh. I helped Rea sit down in the chair on Mila's left. I sat beside Rea as my mum was on Mila's right to help feed her.

Once we were settled, grace was said, the food was passed around like it usually was. I helped dish up for Rea and cut her meat without her having to ask. It wasn't the first time I'd done this for her. She'd broken her arm when we were eighteen, falling when she'd gone ice skating. It was second nature for me to look after her, and I'd fallen into the usual habit of making sure she was looked after.

Only when she went silent and looked from me to her plate did I realise what I'd done.

She just patted my arm and said, "Thank you," before answering Dragon on how she was feeling.

It was a good evening, and it felt right having Rea and Mila with us at the table. She fit in with Abby, Noni, and Avy like she hadn't left.

I wish I didn't have to leave her this evening, but we needed to do this and get rid of as much of this scum as we could or at least hurt them and their bottom line.

Mila was starting to whine a little and was rubbing her eyes. Looking at the clock, I saw it was just after 7:30 p.m., past her bedtime. Not thinking anything of it, I got up, picked her up from the highchair, and tucked her into my chest. I took the bottle mum handed me and sat back down to feed her. Rea was looking at me in surprise.

"You told me to look after her."

I reminded her of her words from last night.

"I did. I'm just surprised at how comfortable Mila is with you. It took Dragon four visits before he could hold her."

I looked across the table at my brother, who nodded.

"It's true. I thought Mila would never let me hold her."

"It's because she knows Uncle Onyx is her dad," Ellie piped up from down the table.

"Ellie, Uncle Milo isn't her dad," Bren tells her sister, who gets a stubborn look on her face.

"Yes, he is, just like Reaper is our dad. They're a little broken, but he'll be her dad for real when they fix their broken. You can see by their colours they belong together."

Her siblings rolled their eyes at their sister, but I couldn't help wishing she was right.

Abby turned to her daughter and asked, "What do you mean you can tell by their colours they belong together?"

The look Ellie gave Abby made me want to laugh. The expression of, *'What is wrong with you all'* on her face was hilarious.

She waved little hands at us and said, "You know! Their colours, like ours, that's how I knew we'd be a family, and I could stop being scared."

"Uh, Ells, you need to explain a bit clearer. We don't understand what colours you mean," Ben told her.

She sighed and rolled her eyes. "You know," she said. "Aunt Avy, Reaper, Mamma A, Sam, Ben, Bren and me have gold all around us just like Grandma Kate and Grandpa Shep. Although his isn't very bright in hospital. I think it's because he's sleeping," she said matter-of-factly.

"Uncle Gunny, Dragon, and Alec are green. Uncle Thor, Uncle Rogue, Aunt Noni and Uncle Bull are purple. Grandpa Dog, Grandma Maggie, Uncle Draco, Uncle Milo, Aunt Rea and Mila are blue. Although Aunt Rea and Uncle Milo have a bit of black in theirs because they need to fix their broken. Can I have more custard, please?" she asked Abby as if she hadn't just dropped a small bomb into the room.

"Huh, I think she means auras," Rea said, looking around the table at the adults whose mouths were slightly agape as they stared at the little girl tucking into her pudding.

"Oh, I forgot one from the family. Aunt Molly is also blue to match Uncle Draco, except when she's mad at him. Then it shimmers with silver," Ellie stated, looking at his brother. "It's very pretty when she's angry at you."

The look on Draco's face at her comment, he didn't know how to respond to that little fact. It was well known that Molly and him were like oil and water. I couldn't help it. I started to laugh, which caused Rea to giggle, until the entire table was laughing. Ellie continued to look at us as though we were all crazy. It was a good way to end the evening. I finished feeding Mila and handed her to Dragon so I could help Rea to my room, but not before I hugged Ellie.

"Never change, baby girl," I told her before going to Rea and picking her up.

I followed Dragon up the stairs thinking that Ellie wasn't wrong. We were broken, but I was going to do my best to fix us.

But first, to settle them in my room for the night and go and cause some mayhem to the ACES drug pipeline.

CHAPTER 6

REA

It had been an interesting day, I thought to myself as I waited for Milo to come back from putting Mila down for the night. I'd cuddled her as much as I could before he'd whisked her away to give her a bath and get her ready for bed.

I was still surprised at how well she'd taken to him and how he'd stepped up to take care of her when he was around. I could feel myself softening toward him. Last night it had been easy to fall into our usual rhythm because of the painkillers and the pain I was in.

I knew we'd need to have a long conversation and put our past to rest before we could begin healing. For now, I was content to wait until the timing was better. I wouldn't be going anywhere for the six weeks it would take for my arm to heal, and after that, there would be physical therapy to strengthen my arm. We would have time. I knew in my heart of hearts that this man was the only man for me, so even though he'd broken me, I was willing to take another chance on him. But before that, he would need to prove that I could trust him again. I had no intention of making this easy on him.

As part of my healing process and before I had been attacked, I had tracked Rebecca down in Bournemouth to confront her about the photos she'd shown me. She'd confirmed it had all been a lie and that she'd tried to talk him out of it, but he had stood firm. She'd apologised for her part in it and was remorseful for what it had cost me.

I'd spent a few hours at her house and had a good chat. I found her to be changed. I understood more about her now and how she'd been brought up. She'd confirmed that her treatment of me stemmed from jealousy, mostly from my family life and then, as the new girl, I'd caught the eye of the most sought-after boy in the school.

This brought the protection of the Crows, and she had envied this.

She'd met and married her husband three years ago. They'd met in an AA meeting after they had been in rehab. He worked in IT, and she'd worked in a local café until their son was born four months ago.

Rebecca and I would never be friends, but I wished her well. I'd left her place feeling slightly better. I knew from experience how the past could play on my emotions and had booked myself back into therapy. I would need to call them tomorrow and see if I could do my next session on the phone as I couldn't get in to see them. My therapist had encouraged me to speak to Milo and bring him in for a session if I felt comfortable with him being there. She didn't think I would fully heal until I'd put the past to rest. I agreed with her I needed to put the past to rest so that I could heal and be the best parent I could be to my daughter. I didn't need the bitterness I felt at Milo's treatment of me to overshadow the rest of my life. It was time to put it all to bed so we could get on with healing, be that together or alone.

Just then, Milo came out of Mila's room carrying a baby monitor and closing the door behind him.

I watched as he headed to the bed where I was sitting. He was still amazing to look at. I could see the physical changes since our last time together. He was far more muscular now, and I knew from when he'd changed his wet shirt after bathing Mila that he had scars that weren't there before. It stood to reason that he would be changed. He couldn't spend fourteen years in the military without being hurt somehow.

Onyx sat on the side of the bed next to me, setting the baby monitor on the bedside table and looked at me with his beautiful dark eyes that had given him his road name.

Sighing, he rubbed his hands down his face before taking my hand that had been resting on the top of the covers in his. I could see he was conflicted.

"I know we need to talk about things, and we will, but it won't be tonight. I also promised myself that I would never lie to you again, so I find myself conflicted in not telling you what I will be up to tonight."

He sighed again, looking at where he was rubbing his thumb across my hand. He'd used to do this when we were dating when he was unsure of something.

I stopped him when I cupped his face with my palm, lifting his face to mine and asking, "Does it have to do with what happened to me?"

"Sort of," he replied. "It's more about the information we managed to get out of the ones that attacked you."

I nodded.

I knew what this was about. I'd had a conversation with the other women about the club, and I knew they didn't run as most MCs. Their women came to their church meetings but only about the business side of the MC. Once that was done, the women left, and that was their choice.

Reaper had offered that they could stay, but they'd said they didn't need to know what the men did to keep them safe. Plus, if they were ever caught, the women would be needed to run the businesses as they now did to keep the money flowing.

"I don't need to know, Milo. Abby and Aunt Maggie told me about how things are done, and if what you are doing tonight is to keep us safe, then I don't want to know. The only thing I need from you is to be safe and for you and the brothers to come home unhurt," I assured him.

His whole body relaxed. I hadn't realised how tense he was. I knew we were both walking on eggshells, but in this, he didn't need to worry. I knew from working in the hospital how bad the drug situation had gotten in our village. And if what they had done to me was the norm, then the ACES needed to be cleared out.

"Okay," he said in relief. "I also want you to know that you don't have to worry about the three that attacked you. They won't be hurting anyone again."

I nodded, not really knowing what to say. Was I relieved that I didn't have to look over my shoulder? *Yes.* Was I happy that they had obviously killed them? *As a doctor, that was harder to swallow.* Shrugging it off, I decided I wouldn't worry about it unless I had to.

"Okay," I replied. "What time do you have to leave tonight?"

"Not until later."

"Well then," I said, patting the bed next to me. "How about we find something to watch on the telly, although I'm not promising I'll stay awake for long now that I've had a pain pill?"

He smiled at me, his face lighting up, making my breath hitch slightly at the look on his face as he got up off the bed and went to get the controls from where they were sitting on his dresser.

Pushing his pillows up on the headboard, he settled down, and we found something to watch. It was some sort of American crime show. I didn't watch much TV, preferring to read, but Milo seemed to enjoy it. I knew I wouldn't be awake much longer. I could already feel my eyelids growing heavy.

I didn't try to stop my body when I naturally moved closer to Milo. He didn't say anything, just lifted his arm and curled it around my shoulders like we'd done it a hundred times before. I rested my good cheek against his chest and let sleep take me away. I'd worry about my growing feelings for him tomorrow. For now, the comfort he offered was familiar, and I needed it more than I needed to breathe.

CHAPTER 7

ONYX

My arm had fallen asleep a while ago from where it was curled around Rea, but I was reluctant to move it. It had been a long time since I'd had this woman in my arms, and I was sorry that I would have to leave soon. I wanted nothing more than to stay in bed with her and hold her in my arms until morning. Unfortunately, the scum that had taken over our village needed to be dealt with.

Sliding her gently from my chest, I tucked the covers around her and made sure her broken arm was supported. I dressed for creating mayhem in black cargos, a black long sleeve t-shirt, and my combat boots. We had balaclavas and gloves in our backpacks.

Making sure that Rea had her next dose of painkillers and water next to the bed, I pressed a gentle kiss to her forehead before grabbing the baby monitor and taking that with me to check on Mila.

Watching her sleep, my heart thudded hard at the thought she wouldn't be mine, if Rea and I couldn't make our peace. Pressing a kiss to my fingertips, I brushed them across her forehead before leaving.

Hurrying into the kitchen, I found Abby, Mum, Avy, Noni, and Aunt Kate sitting at the table. I knew they would stay awake until they heard from Reaper we were safe.

They all turned to look at me as I walked into the kitchen. Worry was clear in their eyes.

Mum got up and hugged me tightly before saying, "Stay safe out there, son."

I nodded but didn't say anything. There was nothing to say. We'd be careful, but things happened as we were all aware. I pressed a kiss to her forehead and hugged her back.

"I will mum, look after my girls," I replied, handing her the baby monitor. I squeezed Abby's shoulder as I left. Our women must be the strongest women I know. I wasn't sure that I would be as calm as them if I had to sit around waiting to hear news about us.

I headed outside to see my brothers similarly dressed as me at the vehicles. The number plates had been muddied, so they couldn't be read, and I saw that the prospects had added a couple of magnetic stickers to the doors portraying different companies. I also didn't recognise a few of the other vehicles, and I wondered where they came from.

Reaper looked up from the large map he'd opened on the bonnet of one of the vehicles when I joined them. He started issuing orders like he was back in the military as soon as we surrounded him.

"Right, you all know what needs to be done. Pull back if there are civilians in sight, but if all you see is ACES, then blow the fuck out of them. I want to take out every one of these labs and warehouses. We know from experience they don't usually have any sort of alarms or CCTV up but make sure you keep your face and hands covered at all times.

"There are a lot of sites to get to tonight, so we're going to have to go into each one alone. I don't like doing that, but if we want to finish the ones around us off tonight, this is how it will have to be. Once we've done this, I'm going to give the routes they travel to someone we know in the NCA and hope to fuck that they can do something about it."

That got nods from all of us surrounding him and waiting on his orders.

He continued, "I don't want to know how, but Blaze managed to get us eight cars that are going for scrap from a friend and had them delivered this afternoon. That means we only have to use four of our cars, and we've disguised them as much as we can. Gunny and Blaze will have to take one of ours and will switch out the magnetic signs once they drop off the package in London.

"Dog and Thor are on security here at the Manor, although all the women are armed, and the alarms will be set once we leave the yard. Check your watches, people. I want you back in this village by 5 a.m. Any issues, contact either Dog, Thor, or myself."

We set our watches so that we are all at the same time.

Reaper looked around at each of us as we confirmed our times and continued. "Gunny, you and Blaze get going. We'll let you know when to drop off the package. The rest of you load up. We leave twenty minutes after them and then at ten-minute intervals. You each have a list of your sites. Those in the cars Blaze found, once you are done, head to the scrap yard. You are expected. Lee Masters is going to pick you up and bring you back here. Good luck. I want every single one of you fuckers back safe and sound by the end of this, or the women are going to have my head."

With that, we dispersed. We each checked our gear to confirm we had all we needed for the night. Then, donning our balaclavas and gloves, we got into the vehicles we'd been assigned.

There was some excitement in the air. I guessed we all missed the adrenaline rush we got just before we headed out into combat. I looked at my list of sites to hit and saw that the first one is a good half-hour drive away. I waited my turn and left when Thor gave me the go-ahead from the gate.

I was just arriving at my first site when I saw a flash in the distance, and flames and smoke went up. It was starting. I quietly closed my door. I was already armed and had my knives which I preferred as they were quieter than a gun. Grabbing the explosives I needed, I headed into the dark.

Ten minutes later, I was driving away, I watched a flash behind me followed by a satisfying boom, and I couldn't help but grin as I saw the fire behind me. Five more to go. It was going to be a good night.

You didn't want to fuck with the Crow family. Especially one of their women.

Dawn was just breaking as I pulled into the family parking lot. I'd been driving one of our vehicles. On the way home, I'd stopped in a lay-by and removed and destroyed the magnetic signs, cleaned off the number plates, vacuumed the car with the small vacuum cleaner, and wiped down the interior with wipes kept in the glove compartment. The car smelled as if it had been newly valeted. Dragon pulled up next to me, and I wandered over to him as he got out.

I grinned when I smelt the interior of the vehicle he had used.

"Freshly valeted? Nice," I grinned at him.

"Got to keep the women happy about the state of their vehicles," he agreed, returning my grin and patting the side of the vehicle he'd used.

We each took the backpacks we'd used to carry everything in and headed towards the abattoir and the underground bunker that housed our guns and hardware.

Nodding at Skinny, who was on lookout, we headed to where the rest of the brothers and prospects were already taking stock of what we'd used and what needed re-stocking.

"All good?" Reaper asked as we got closer.

"Yep, they should be nice and toasty on this fresh morning," I replied, smiling.

There was a snort of laughter from within the room as the others grinned at my choice of words. Dragon and I handed our bags to Bond when he asked for them.

He looked at Reaper after adding everything back into stock, "We're going to have to stock up with more explosives if this carries on, Reaper," he advised.

Reaper nodded after checking the list he was given.

"Thanks, Bond. I'll speak to Noni and have her call Old man O'Shea."

Bull protested loudly at his words and said unhappily, "Ah hell, no, Reap. Why Noni?"

Reaper looked at Bull with his eyebrows raised at Bull's protest, and the man looked stubbornly back at him. I guessed his feelings for Noni outweighed the wrath of his President. I smirked at my thoughts and wondered how Noni felt about this.

"Because Bull, she's his ex-daughter-in-law and not by her choice either, and the old goat loves her. He doesn't trust the rest of us, and he'll only deal with her. Who do you think got us the hardware you've been using?"

Bull tilted his head down at the reprimand but didn't look happy with the fact that Noni was brokering our deals in illegal arms. Truth be told, none of us was happy about it, but we also knew that old man O'Shea wouldn't let anything happen to Noni. He'd cut off his right arm before he allowed her to be hurt in any way.

Reaper's phone rang, and he pulled it out of his pocket to check who it was.

"Gunny," he answered, walking off.

Rogue was leaning against the abattoir wall listening to the conversation, and I could see he wanted to say something but was torn. Sighing, he stood upright from where he'd been leaning. Rogue wasn't one to say much. He preferred to be in the background or ride his bike unless it involved giving his sister a hard time.

He was a restless soul, and I often wondered what it would take for him to be content staying in one place. I knew once we'd sorted the ACES out, he would be on the back of his bike on a road trip. It's why he'd been made the Road Captain.

"Bull," Rogue drawled softly, "I don't usually get involved in my sister's shit. But I like you, and Noni has been through enough heartache in the last two years, so I'm going to give you some advice, and you can take it or leave it.

"If you want any type of relationship to happen with Noni, then you need to lay off the O'Sheas. She'll choose them if it's a choice between you and them. Every time!

"That won't change until she feels like she can trust you, and you give her a reason not to put them first. One thing you have to understand about Noni is that she is loyal to her core. She doesn't have a lot of friends, but once you are in her circle of trust, she'll do anything for you. And the O'Sheas have always been there for her. She loves them, and they love her. The only reason she isn't still married is that Rhett forced the divorce. He didn't want her to waste her life waiting for him while he was inside. You're going to have a hard road to travel when it comes to my sister, but I can tell you that she will be worth every minute you put into winning her over."

There was silence as Bull stood there, taking in what Rogue was laying out. Those of us that had grown up with her knew what he meant. We thought it came from their mother leaving them when they were young. Noni's way of proving she was not her mother was to always put those in her circle first and never leave them. Just like it was Rogue's nature to always go searching.

"Are you getting what I'm laying down, brother?" Rogue asked seriously.

You could see the indecision on Bull's face, but I knew that Rogue was right. If Bull wanted anything with Noni, he would need to let her still do what she needed to do with the O'Sheas.

Bull jerked his chin up in acknowledgement, "I get you, Rogue."

"Good, brother, good."

Reaper came back from taking Gunny's call. He stopped when he saw the way Bull and Rogue were facing off.

Rogue waved a hand to Reaper. "Continue, Pres. We're good here."

"Right, Church at 2 pm this afternoon, don't be late. We'll catch up, and you can fill us in on your night. Gunny and Blaze dropped the package and are heading out to pick up Beverley. I'm bushed, and I have a warm woman waiting for me in bed, so I'll see you fuckers later," he said before walking off.

Draco looked at me as he came out of the bunker with the prospects. "Head in, brother. Rogue and I'll secure this."

Nodding, I said my goodbyes to the others and headed to the house. I knew that Mila would be up soon, but I may still be able to catch a few hours' sleep until then.

Walking into the kitchen, I saw a note resting against the vase of flowers in the middle of the kitchen table.

Milo,

Dad and I have Mila in our wing. Don't rush in the morning, I have cover in the café so I won't be going in.

Love you

Mum

I smiled as I read the note and headed up the stairs to my wing. Opening the door quietly, I saw that Rea was still sleeping, her hair spread out over the pillows. Something settled in my chest as I watched her for a moment before getting undressed and going to the bathroom.

I knew I had a long road to fix what I broke between us. I could only hope that she would eventually forgive me for my stupidity.

I grabbed a quick shower and headed to bed. Laying down, my hand found Rea's lying on the bed between us, and I fell asleep with my fingers curled around hers.

CHAPTER 8

REA

I groaned loudly as I woke up with a jolt. The nightmare that had me in its grip finally released me. Opening my eyes, I let out another moan as my entire body protested in pain at my sudden movement. The pain that shot through me took my breath away. Tears sprang in my eyes in response to the pain passing through my body.

I felt movement from next to me and realised someone was holding my hand. Turning my head to see Milo waking up, I saw his tired dark eyes.

He sat up, still gripping my hand in his.

"Are you in pain, babe?"

"Yeah," I nodded. "Can you help me up? I need the bathroom and another pain pill, then you can go back to sleep."

"Give me a minute," he said as he got up and came around to my side of the bed. He shook the pain pills out into his hand before handing them to me, followed by a bottle of water.

He grimaced slightly in sympathy as he looked at my face.

I touched my cheek gently before saying, "Second day, so I guess the bruising is looking pretty bad now, huh?"

"It's not good, babe. On a scale of one to ten, how much pain are you in?"

I snorted slightly and looked up at him.

"About a twenty," I replied as I tried to swing my legs off the bed but ended up holding my breath as the agony of my bruised ribs caused black spots to appear in front of my eyes.

"Jesus, Sugar, let me help you up. That's why I'm here, so you don't have to do this alone. Now, slowly, I'm going to help you stand, and we'll get you to the bathroom. Okay?"

"Yeah," I said softly and opened my eyes to see his dark with concern as he put his arms under mine and bent his legs to lift me up off the bed. I whimpered slightly and leaned my weight against his body, sighing at the familiar feel of his arms as they came around me and held me gently against him.

"Ready?" he asked.

If it wasn't for my bladder screaming at me to empty it, I could quite happily have stayed where I was.

Instead, I replied, "Yes, let's go."

I thought it would bother me having him help me to the bathroom and then to get situated when we realised I couldn't lower myself to the toilet without my ribs causing me agony. Once I was situated, he left and waited outside the bathroom door.

"Call me when you're done."

I'd cheekily saluted him with my good arm and replied, "Sir, yes, Sir."

I made him laugh as he left the room, muttering, *cheeky brat*.

Finishing up, I called out to him. He got me up and to the sink with little problem, and I washed my hand and stared at the damage to my face in the mirror. The bruises were completely out now, and I knew my face would be a riot of colour in a few days as they started healing.

"Do you want me to run you a hot bath to try to ease your muscles?" Milo asked, watching me from the doorway.

"Aren't you tired?" I asked.

"Yeah, but I can sleep later. We only have church this afternoon, and it's only just gone 6:30. You'll feel better if you can relax your muscles and even catch another couple of hours of sleep," he explained.

"What about Mila?" I questioned.

"Mum and Dad have her in their wing. There was a note left on the kitchen table when I came in not to worry about her and to take our time this morning."

I wasn't sure how I felt about that. On the one hand, I knew Mila was as safe as could be with Maggie. Still, on the other, I was the only one who had ever looked after Mila other than my neighbour, and even that was only for a few hours.

Milo must have seen the look on my face because he said quickly, "Why don't you relax for half an hour in the bath and once you're done, I'll take you downstairs to see her. I can catch a few hours after I've done that."

"Okay," I agreed, slowly turning towards the bath.

Milo hurried in, saying as he walked towards the bath, "Let me get it started, then I'll wrap your arm for you."

Now that the pain was abating, thanks to the wonderful medication I'd been given, I noticed he was shirtless in only a pair of boxer shorts. I couldn't help but become aroused as I watched how the muscles in his back bunched and released as he added Epsom salts into the water and swirled his hands around. Then the muscles in his thighs flexed as he stood up and shook his hands out. I bit my lip to hold in the whimper that wanted to escape. I quickly raised my eyes to the ceiling as he turned back to me.

"You okay, babe?" he asked, watching me from where he was standing next to the bath.

I nodded slightly, not wanting him to know how much he was affecting me.

'Bloody hell, you'd think with the amount of pain I'm in, my body wouldn't get aroused.'

Milo didn't say anything but came over to help me wrap up my cast, so it didn't get wet.

He cleared his throat, and I lifted my eyes up to see him watching me. I raised my eyebrows in question.

"Rea, are you going to be good with me helping you into the bath or do you need me to go get one of the other women?" he questioned.

I thought about it. My body was nothing like it was when we'd been together. I now had stretch marks on my breasts and stomach. A pooch from carrying Mila that, no matter how many sit-ups I did, stayed the same. It was not something that had ever worried me, though. They were reminders that I'd carried another person in my body.

Shrugging, I thought it would be a test to see how serious he was about fixing us. If there was even a blink of disgust from him about the changes to my body from carrying a child, not his, I would know, and I'd make plans to get out of there.

"You can help me," I replied quietly.

He took a shocked breath, and his dark eyes widened in surprise.

"Really?" he asked.

His face showed his shock that I'd allow him to see me naked.

I lifted my shoulders slightly in a shrug before saying, "Yeah, it's not like you've never seen me naked before. It seems pointless waking one of the others."

"Okay, if you're uncomfortable at all, just say, and I'll go wake up one of the other women to give you a hand," he assured me.

I nodded in agreement and told him, "You're going to have to help me get out of this shirt, though.

Nodding, he unbuttoned the flannel shirt I was wearing and gently pulled the sleeves down and off my arms. Soon I was standing in only my knickers, and I lowered my eyes. I had made it out like it wasn't a big deal for him to see me naked, but now that it was happening, I was suddenly unsure. Milo went down to his knees, his hands on my hips as he pulled my underwear down and lifted my feet. His hands held me steady as he pulled them off each foot. I thought I heard him groan something out, but I couldn't be sure.

He lifted his head up, his eyes darkened, and he took note of what was in front of him. He licked his lips as he looked at my naked chest, and I shuddered slightly in response. I knew exactly how those lips felt on my nipples, nipples that were rock-hard nubs as his breath brushed across them. My body swayed forward, and Milo's hands tightened on my hips as his eyes closed, hiding his hunger from my gaze. Standing up, he steadied me. His eyes met mine, and he swallowed hard.

"So beautiful," he muttered with a growl as he traced a finger around my nipple. I whimpered slightly and bit my lip at how good it felt to have his hands on my naked body again.

I wish I'd held that whimper in because it seemed to act as a reminder that he wasn't meant to be touching me because he jerked his hand back and clenched it into a fist.

"Let's get you in the bath," he said with a groan before picking me up and gently putting me in the bath. I sighed and closed my eyes in bliss as I felt the heat seep into my abused, painful muscles. Then, leaning back, I rested my head against the towel Milo tucked behind my neck.

I opened my eyes when Milo spoke, his eyes averted from where I lay in the bath as he picked up my dirty clothes and deposited them in the laundry basket.

"I'll be back to help you out. I'm just going to get you something else to wear."

"Okay," I replied softly.

His eyes flicked to mine, and he licked his lips, pausing as if he wanted to say something before closing his eyes tightly, his hands fisted on his hips.

My eyes lowered and widened as I saw evidence of his hard length, showcased in his tight grey boxers.

'I guess he didn't mind the changes to my body,'

With a small grin, I closed my eyes again. I was unsure if it was the pain pill or if Milo still found me attractive, but I was suddenly feeling much better about life.

CHAPTER 9

ONYX

Helping Rea get undressed and in the bath had been sheer torture. I'd been hard-pressed to keep my hands to myself as I'd undressed her. I could feel my cock hardening as I undid the flannel shirt she was wearing, *my* flannel shirt, one button at a time. Revealing glimpses of her soft, full breasts. I was hard as a rock by the time I helped her off with it.

Not sure which was worse, helping her remove *my* shirt from her body or removing her underwear. Not that I'd been able to keep my hands to myself, I'd tried, but when I'd seen her hard nipples, I hadn't been able to help myself. Instead, I'd had to run my fingers around them.

Her body wasn't the same as the last time we'd been together. I hadn't expected it to be. For me, the changes it had gone through carrying not only our child for five months and then Mila were amazing. Was she heavier, with more curves now? Yes. Did she carry marks from her pregnancies? Yes.

To me, they were a beautiful reminder of what her body was capable of.

'Fuck, I wanted to suck and kiss every part of her. Worship her body until she no longer felt insecure about any part of herself,'

I'd thought this when I ran my finger around her nipple.

Only when she whimpered quietly did I realise what I was doing and cursed myself. Here she was in pain, and all I could think about was fucking her. I was a god damned idiot, perving on a hurt woman, a woman that was hurt because of us. I'd helped her into the bath and smiled a little as she groaned at the heat warming her sore muscles. Tucking a towel behind her head so that she could lay back and relax.

I'd held back a growl as her breasts bobbed out of the water as she laid back. I had needed to get out of there before I fucked up and did something to put us back again to where we'd been a couple of months ago. Hurriedly I'd left the bathroom once I'd told her where I was going and willed my cock to go down.

Gathering up clothing for her, including another of my flannel shirts, this time in blue, I put them on the bed before checking my phone. Not seeing any messages from my brothers, I checked the time and saw that Rea had been in the bath for over twenty minutes.

Knocking on the bathroom door, I asked, "You ready to get out, Sugar?"

"Yeah, please."

Grabbing the large bath towel from the radiator where it was warming, I gritted my teeth because I would have to help her get dressed.

"Torture, pure torture," I muttered to myself.

Walking in, I tried not to let my eyes travel over Rea, where she sat waiting for me to help her out.

I pulled the plug and watched as the water ran out of the bath. Keeping my eyes on hers, I saw her looking at me with amusement, and a small smile tipped up the corners of her lips as her eyes drifted down towards my crotch.

"Ignore him, babe. He has a mind of his own. He was always like that around you," I admitted, returning her smile.

She let out a small laugh and grinned up at me.

"I don't mind. It makes me happy to know you still want me like that."

"Never stopped, Sugar. I've always wanted you."

Her face stayed soft as she asked, "So, how do you want to do this?"

Realising I was still standing there holding the towel, and the bath was nearly empty of water, I apologised, "Sorry, Sugar. I'm going to put my arms under your armpits and lift you. I will be as gentle as possible, but you may still hurt some."

"Okay," she agreed, lifting her arms as high as she could, which wasn't that high due to the damage to her ribs.

Putting my arms under the armpits, I lifted. She hissed slightly as her ribs protested the movement. I wrapped her in a warm bath sheet, picked her up bridal style and walked into my bedroom.

Sitting her down on the bed, I picked up a towel I had left there with her clothes and started drying her. Once done, I picked up her knickers and held them out for her to put her feet into before pulling them up her legs. I pressed a kiss to her knee without thinking. I froze when I realised what I'd done.

Groaning, I pressed my forehead to the towel on her thighs.

"I'm sorry," I whispered. "I keep forgetting that we no longer have a relationship like this."

Rea sighed, and her good hand rested on my head. She started running her fingers through my hair.

"Milo, this is going to be strange for both of us. We were together for a long time. We're both bound to do things without thinking. I did last night when I lay on your chest watching TV like we used to before you left. Will we be able to fix what was broken? Honestly, I don't know. But I know that we were friends long before we were lovers. So why don't we start there and stop beating ourselves up when we do something without thinking, okay?" she said, tilting my head up so I could meet her gaze.

"Okay," I agreed before helping her on with her leggings and the flannel. For my sanity, I put the flannel on her over the towel before pulling the towel out from under it.

Grabbing a brush, I helped her with her hair before taking her to the stairs. She was moving much easier since her bath. I only picking her up when we got to the stairs. I made sure she was comfortable on the couch in the lounge before going to the kitchen. I grabbed a couple of heat bags from the pile in the basket kept in the hallway. Making us each a cup of tea while they heated up. Taking them back to where she waited, I tucked them under her back and hips to help keep her muscles warm.

"Thanks, Milo, that feels good."

"No problem, babe. I'm just going to get our tea, and I'll be back," I replied before heading back to the kitchen.

Putting her mug of tea on a side table, I made sure she could reach it before tucking one of the throws around her and settling in one of the recliners. It wasn't long before I was asleep. It had been a long night and an interesting morning.

I was woken up by a soft murmur of voices having a whispered conversation.

"I can change her for you," Ben offered quietly.

"Are you sure?" I could hear the doubt in Rea's voice.

He gave a little chuckle before replying.

"Yeah, Rea, I know how to change nappies. Both Bren and I had to learn quickly. I changed Ellie's nappies from the day she was born until she was potty trained. Trust me, there isn't much I don't know about looking after babies," Ben answered.

I heard rustling. Cracking my eyes open, I watched as Ben picked up Mila's nappy bag and got her changed in short order.

'I hate his parents. The fuckers need putting down.'

I thought this as I watched him with Mila. Keeping her entertained by making faces until she was changed.

We needed to get Ben and his sisters sorted, so they didn't live in limbo expecting to be sent back to their waste of space parents. They were fantastic kids, much of that because of Ben and his strength and what he was willing to do to keep them together.

"Huh, I think you're faster than me at that," Rea told him with a small grin when he handed her Mila and a bottle once he was done.

"Better than Onyx anyway. You should have seen him the first night you were here. Nana Maggie had to rescue him," he snickered, his eyes shooting to mine as he grinned big.

"Cheeky little fucker," I said, jumping up from my chair and grabbing him in a headlock. It didn't take long, and he had me on the ground where we wrestled until he called uncle.

"Okay, okay, I give up," Ben panted.

I lay next to him on the carpet and looked up at the clapping coming from the doorway. Tilting my head back, I saw Reaper and Dragon in the doorway.

"He's getting pretty good," I said proudly.

"He is," Reaper agreed, smiling. "Church in ten, don't be late."

I threw him a salute, "Will do, Pres."

Getting up off the floor, I pulled Ben up with me, hugged him, and ruffled his hair.

"Keep it up, Ben. Whatever you're doing is working. I had to work pretty hard to keep you down. Next session at the gym, we'll work on your holds, yeah?"

"Thanks, Onyx."

He beamed at me before leaving the room with a little bounce in his step.

"I love those kids," Rea said with a smile. "I hope their home situation is sorted soon, and they get to stay here."

"Yeah," I agreed. "We all do. I think Abby may just kidnap them if they don't get to stay. I'm heading out to church. Is there anything you need before I go?"

Rea shook her head. "Nah, Bren and Ellie are coming to keep me company. Avy and Noni sent a message to let me know the women aren't meeting with you guys today, so they'll be here soon. Go, we'll be fine."

I still hesitated as I stood there watching her feed Mila. It was a beautiful picture, and I couldn't stop the dart of regret that went through me at what I'd missed.

I was shaken out of my thoughts by Ellie and Bren coming through the door. I got a hug from both of them before they settled down with books and drawings ready to keep Rea company but not before asking Rea if she needed anything.

"See," Rea said with a smile. "I'm well looked after."

"Okay."

Bending, I pressed a kiss to Mila's forehead and Rea's before I left the room.

Looking back when I reached the door, Ellie was smiling widely at me, holding her fingers in the form of a heart. She mouthed, "Nearly blue," before giggling and going back to her colouring.

Shaking my head, I left the room, but I did it smiling.

CHAPTER 10

ONYX

When I arrived, the clubhouse was heaving with the entire MC, other than the prospects at the gate.

Heading to the bar, I saw Avy behind it.

"Don't you get tired of serving punters, Av?" I asked her as she handed me a bottle of beer without me having to ask.

"Nope, I like being behind the bar," she replied as I took a drink from the bottle she had handed me.

I paused to read the label before I took another drink.

Avy was watching me with a twinkle in her eye.

"It's good," I said while taking another drink.

"Does he know?" I motioned with my chin to Draco, who had a bottle in his hand.

"Nope, I tore some of his label off before I gave it to him." Avy grinned, her blue eyes twinkling mischievously. "He deserved it after turning his nose up at the homebrew Molly had in her kitchen," she said with a chuckle.

"I'm surprised he hasn't seen the brewery, with the amount of time he spends over there," I said, handing my empty bottle back to Avy.

I noted that everyone had tried one, and all the bottles were standing empty. Looking around, I noticed the women were all watching Draco as he finished his.

My comment made Avy laugh. Leaning over the bar towards me, she whispered, "It's in the barn on her five acres, she keeps it locked, and Hawk told me the last time they were over there, Molly met them with a shotgun and told Draco he wasn't welcome and she'd shoot him if he tried to come onto her five acres. She then let Hawk in the gate."

Avy was crying with laughter, as were Noni and Abby, who had joined us when Avy had leant over the bar.

I grinned. I couldn't wait to meet Molly. My brother deserved to be taken down a peg or two. I was looking forward to watching the fallout.

Draco finished his conversation, held up his empty bottle and called out to Avy, "This beer is really good, Avy. Who makes it?"

All the women burst into laughter as Avy answered, "Oh, just a local brewery that I use to supply the pub. I'll let them know that you thought it was good."

Draco looked around with a confused expression at our grinning faces before shrugging and putting his empty bottle on the bar.

Reaper let out a piercing whistle and called out, "Crows head to Church, ladies, we'll see you after as there is no business or finance to talk about today. Avy, make sure the prospects stock up on that beer will you?" he ordered with a chuckle.

Avy saluted him with a big smile, "Will do, Reap."

Walking into our new Church was a little surreal. For as long as I could remember, meetings had always been held in the house. It was only when Reaper took over as President that we moved into the old barn at the back of the property. We'd needed to grow the MC and couldn't continue to use the main house. Not with the growing number of families now residing there.

I ran my hand over our meeting table. It was a thing of beauty. Hard to believe that Abby's fourteen-year-old Sam had carved and built it.

We settled into our seats, Reaper at the head with Draco to his left and Dragon to his right. I sat on Dragon's right and Rogue on Draco's left. The came Bull next to Rogue, Hawk next to me and Navy next to

Hawk. My dad's generation filled the bottom of the table. The only ones missing this meeting were Gunny and Shep.

Reaper called the meeting to order.

"Right, you wankers, let's hear updates on last night. Were there any problems?"

Resounding No's came from around the table. It had all gone as smoothly as clockwork.

"No problems, but I had a shit ton of fun," Navy said with a grin. "Any chance there are more labs to blow up?"

Laughter filled the room. We all felt like that. It had been good to get rid of more of the labs, even if they were out of our area.

"Sorry, Navy, no more labs that we know of. That could change depending on what Gunny's woman has to say. They'll be arriving this evening. We'll let her settle in and have another meeting Monday evening. Your arses better be here at 19:00 hours. Keep your eyes open for trouble over the next couple of weeks.

"I need a rotation on Abby when she drops off and collects the kids from school. There are some rumblings from Ben and the girl's parents."

"Let's just make them disappear," Dragon seethed angrily. "Those kids have been through enough."

"I agree with you, brother. Unfortunately, everyone knows where they are living, and if the parents disappear, it will bring heat down on us." Reaper scowled, his face tight with anger. "They're not getting my kids, though, so it may still come to that."

"We can make it look like an accidental drug overdose," Bull added. "I'd be happy to do it, to keep them here safe. You know my background, Skinny, and I grew up like them. We joined the military to get out. It's what saved us from ending up like our parents."

"I know, brother. Thank you for the offer," Reaper acknowledged. "I hope it doesn't come to that, but I'm willing to put it back on the table if it does. Looking at Dragon, he added, "Dragon can you organise the rotation, including the prospects?"

"Will do Reap, already on my list," Dragon acknowledges.

"Now that I've brought up the prospects, do any of you have concerns regarding them? Their three months are nearly up, and we'll need to vote soon on patching them in?"

"No concerns from me," I answered.

"If you could get Cairo to wear a shirt, it would be appreciated," Bull griped. "If I have to hear Noni say another thing about his body, he may not have one to flex around the women," he muttered, scowling.

His moaning set off another round of laughter.

"You do know she only does it because you hate it, right?" Rogue chuckled, punching Bull on the shoulder.

Bull grinned sheepishly, "I know, but fuck Rogue, your sister is hard to pin down."

"Yeah, you're going to have to work your arse off to get my daughter to give you a chance. I don't envy you. My baby has seen a lot of hurt in her life. But if you can get her to take that chance, a more loyal woman you won't find. That being said, if you add to that hurt, as old as I am, I'll put you down," Thor said with a serious look on his face.

For his age, he was still fit and was only a little smaller than Bull. It would be a close thing if they ever decided to go at it.

"If you're all finished discussing Bull and Noni's love life can we finish this meeting? I have a woman and kids to get to and a father to visit in the hospital," Reaper boomed, calling the meeting back to order.

A round of *sorry Pres* echoed around the room.

"Now that I have all your attention again. The women are planning a barbeque for

Sunday to welcome Beverly. Get with them to see if they need anything. I'm heading to the hospital to see my dad. I wish the fucker would wake up," he muttered a little grumpily. "If there is nothing else, then this meeting is adjourned, get out of here but remember to stay safe, eyes open, and nobody rides alone," he added, banging the table with the gavel ending the meeting.

We walked back out into the main room of the clubhouse. The single guys headed to the bar, now manned by a prospect and to play darts. I knew they would probably head out to check out the clubs Liam wanted us to invest in, later tonight.

Reaper had brought it to the table a month ago but had wanted us to check them out first. He wanted more information on the areas, clientele and footfall. Bella, Avy and Noni were going over the books for each club. We'd only invest if they gave it the go-ahead.

From what I understood from previous conversations, it looked like two were good, but one had books that didn't match the amount of footfall that went through it. It seemed like someone was skimming the books or something else was happening.

I wasn't going to worry about any of that for now. I wanted to spend time with my girls.

Walking into the kitchen, Aunt Kate was at the counter pouring a glass of wine, and the kitchen table was groaning with cold meats, salad and bread.

"Hi, Aunt Kate," I said, surprised to see her at home so early.

She turned from where she'd been pouring glasses of wine and smiled. She looked more relaxed than I'd seen her in a while.

"Hello, Milo love. It's been decided that it's movie night tonight. Help yourself to food and drink and come to the family room. Don't worry about Rea. She already has a plate," she said with a beaming smile.

"Um, Aunt Kate, how much wine have you had?" I asked with concern looking at the clock and seeing it was only just after five o'clock.

She let out a tinkling laugh before joyously informing me, "I haven't had any yet, Milo. This is my first glass. I'm just happy and celebrating. Shep woke up this morning. We didn't let anyone know because the doctors wanted to make sure that all was okay.

"He kicked me out when he found out I'd been there all day. Reaper and Abby are with him until later, and then I'll go back for the night. Cairo is driving me so I can have a glass of wine."

"That's fantastic news Aunt Kate," I said, picking her up in a hug before gently putting her back on her feet, making sure she was steady before stepping back.

"Yes, it is. I can't wait to bring him home. Now, dish up and head to the family room where the kids are setting up the movie," she gushed happily and left the room with a spring in her step that had been missing the last two months.

I hurriedly piled up my plate and went to the family room. It was packed. The kids were all lying on the floor on pillows and beanbags, and they all had full plates of food. Rea was still on the couch. She had a plate balanced on her knees but scrunched up her legs a little, so I could sit on the end. She smiled at me as I stepped over the kids to get to her. Mila was lying on a play mat next to Bren.

"What are we watching?" I inquired as I sat down.

Ice Age was shouted out.

I grinned, settling down to be entertained. Finishing my plate, I put it on the table next to me. Pulling Rea's feet onto my legs, I absently massaged them, my attention on the movie and the antics of the characters. It was only when I heard a small groan that I looked away and realised what I was doing. Rea's head was turned to watch the TV, but she turned to me when I stopped rubbing her feet and kicked up, gently nudging me.

"Don't stop. It feels good," Rea whispered softly with a small smile.

Smiling back at her, I continued rubbing her feet and went back to watching the movie.

It was the most relaxed I'd seen Rea since I'd brought her here from the hospital.

CHAPTER 11

REA

Lying in bed Sunday night thinking over the last couple of days, while I waited for Milo to finish putting Mila down for the night, I thought about how much things had changed for me over the last four months since the Crow MC had come back into my life.

Most of it was good. I'd missed being in their lives. The part I was unsure about was Milo and how he was slowly becoming important to me again.

I was still sleeping in his room, in his bed, even if I was moving easier than I had three days ago. I wasn't sure if continuing to stay in his room was a good thing or not. We'd fallen into our earlier friendship from when we were younger. It felt good to have my friend back. I'd still not forgiven him for the pain he'd caused me. We'd been putting off talking about anything serious. I didn't think either of us wanted to break the status quo we were currently in.

My problem, however, was my libido. After it being dead for years, just a few nights in the same bed with Milo, it had woken up.

Every morning I woke to find myself wrapped around him. He never said anything, and he didn't push me away even though I knew the hard cock I felt against the thigh that always seemed to creep over his hips couldn't be comfortable for him. Just thinking of him and the changes that time had made to his body was getting me hot.

To take my mind off thinking of Milo and my need to constantly want to jump him, I let my mind wander to the arrival of Beverly. Beverly and Gunny, along with Blaze, had arrived late that afternoon, and her arrival had caused quite a stir among the MC members and family.

Having heard of her history with drugs and her life, she was not what I'd been expecting at all. Going by the reaction of the others, I don't think anyone was expecting her to look like she did. I mean, I'd figured she must be pretty because Alec had good bone structure and was a good-looking lad. However, the woman who'd gotten out of Gunny's Range Rover was stunningly gorgeous.

They'd been delayed and hadn't arrived Saturday evening as expected, instead arriving at lunchtime on Sunday just in time for the barbecue.

We'd all been sitting on the patio by the barbecue area built behind the clubhouse. The men were barbecuing, and Avy, Noni, Maggie and myself were slowly making inroads into the jugs of mojito Avy had made. I was feeling pretty relaxed between the alcohol, the warm sun, and the eye candy around the barbecue. Even Mila cooperated as she was asleep in her pushchair beside me.

It was Navy's face that first alerted me that we had company. His jaw dropped as he gaped. I'd turned slowly in my chair to look over my shoulder to see what had him so enthralled.

"Holy moly," I said softly, patting Avy's hand. She looked at me with questioning eyes. "Gunny's back," I whispered. Still looking confused, she too turned and looked.

"Holy cannoli, she's stunning," Avy muttered in awe and hit Noni's leg to get her attention.

Noni muttered, "What the hell is wrong with you two? Then with a drawn out, "Fuuuck, Aunt Maggie, have you seen her? The men are going to go gaga."

"Noni, language," Maggie grumbled, then we heard her say with a small chuckle, "Well, well, Gunny, you dirty dog," before she got up from her chair and walked over to meet them.

The stunning woman walking towards us with her hand tucked into Gunny's was a little shorter than Gunny's six foot, with long, healthy-looking red hair that fell well past her shoulders, high cheekbones, and full lips. She had the classic hourglass shape of big breasts, a tiny waist and wide hips. She wore a white off-shoulder gipsy shirt tucked into a pair of jeans that were rolled up at the ankle showing off a golden anklet. On her feet were flat gladiator sandals.

Before Maggie got to them, we watched as her face broke into a stunning smile, and she took off towards where the teenagers had been playing football. Alec's face beamed with a huge grin when he realised who it was running to him, and he opened his arms wide as she threw her arms around him before peppering his face with kisses.

I would have thought that a lad like him would be embarrassed by her affection, but he just laughed and hugged her back tight.

"It's good to see you, mum," we heard him say.

"You too, baby. I've missed you so much. Talking on the phone isn't the same as seeing you," she replied, wiping the tears from her cheeks.

It was beautiful to watch. As was the hug Gunny and Alec had exchanged when he'd made his way over to them. They'd chatted for a bit before Gunny brought Beverly over to meet the rest of us. It was only when she took off her sunglasses that you realised she wasn't as young as her appearance made her out to be. Her eyes, while warm, held shadows.

She was warm and friendly, with a great sense of humour. She made no secret that she thought Gunny was the best thing that had ever happened to her. I knew she was serious about staying sober when she declined Avy's drink.

"Thank you for the offer Avy, but I'll stick to a soft drink. Now that I'm here, though, I need to tell you all how wonderful it is to finally meet you all. Alec talks about you all every time I speak to him. I appreciate all you have done for him and wanted to thank you for showing him what a good female role model is," Beverly stated with a smile, her eyes a little teary, "God knows I've been a terrible one."

Maggie reached over and patted her hand, "Not a terrible one, hun. Maybe a little lost, but you did what you had to do to keep him safe, and he knows that. He's only ever said good things about you."

The tears that had been brimming spilt over, and she wiped at her cheeks.

"Thank you, Maggie, that means a lot coming from you. I know how much you've helped Gunny with him."

"Here," I said softly, grabbing the box of tissues from under Mila's pram and handing them to her.

We'd been so engrossed in our conversation that none of us had heard Gunny coming over until he demanded, "Why is she crying? What have you said to her?"

Beverly took his hand that he'd placed on her shoulder and pressed a kiss to the back of it.

"They haven't done anything, hun. It's me getting emotional thanking them for helping with Alec when I couldn't."

His face softened as he looked at her and ran his finger down her cheek.

"You don't have to thank us for looking out for family, darling. I've told you this."

"I know," she answered. "But I still wanted all the women to know it was appreciated."

"Good, you've done that, so stop with the crying and come and get some food," he muttered gruffly.

Maggie snickered. "Tears still make you uncomfortable, Gunny?"

"They do when they come from the woman I love," he replied.

Pulling Beverly up from her chair where she'd sat since joining us, they walked over to the food tables.

"Aw, Gunny, you have a heart."

Noni smirked with a laugh as they left and then laughed harder at his response when he held up his hand with the middle finger raised.

It had been a good day, I'd forgotten how warm the MC was as a family, and the new recruits fitted in well. There was a lot of celebrating going on today. Reaper's Dad, Shep, had finally woken up and seemed to be doing okay. I'd offered to go in and check on him, but Milo had shot that down, stating I could go when I was no longer black and blue. He had a point it wouldn't go down well with Shep if I turned up looking like I did.

I'd spent most of the Sunday ensconced in my chair, watching them carrying on around me. Everyone seemed more than happy to fetch and carry food and drink to me. I hardly saw Mila. If she wasn't with Milo, she was with Maggie. Not that it bothered her, but she was equally as comfortable with the rest of the MC.

There was an interesting dynamic going on between Bull and Noni. He'd have his work cut out for him there to get her to give him a chance. By all accounts, Noni was still hurting from her divorce and from what I understood from Avy was still in love with her ex-husband. I could sympathise. I knew what it was like when the man in your life made decisions to supposedly make your life easier.

I just hoped she would give him a chance and put her past behind her. Easier said than done. I knew that. I was living proof of how hard it could be.

I was hoping that the information Beverly had to give them tomorrow would end all the drugs in our village and that we could all go back to living semi-normal lives again.

I was sure we'd all get an update tomorrow after Church. It wasn't like the men to keep information from us if it pertained to keeping us safe.

CHAPTER 12

REAPER

I'm sitting in Church waiting for the men to arrive after eating supper at the main house. I grinned a little, thinking of the shakeup that Beverly and Gunny had caused. To say that the entire MC had been stunned when he'd walked in with her was an understatement. Blaze had been smirking at the surprise on all our faces when he'd followed behind Gunny and Beverly.

Not only had she been easy on the eyes, she was also laid back, had a great sense of humour and made no bones about the fact that she loved Gunny and Alec. Considering the life she had led, I had expected her to be harder. Oh, don't get me wrong, I think she could be if she was pushed. She'd be pretty bloody hard and not think twice about putting you in your place if you threatened hers. She had done it to protect Alec when he was ten.

I got what Gunny meant when he said she was close to her son; you could see it in how they interacted. Still, I would keep an eye on her and make sure she was as she seemed.

The men slowly began trickling in. Gunny and Beverly were the last ones in. She was carrying a large envelope.

Gunny pulled out the chair next to his.

"Thanks, honey," she said with a smile.

"Boys."

She acknowledged the rest of us with a grin, her eyes crinkling at the corners with hidden amusement at some of the looks she was getting from the men.

We snickered when Gunny's hand connected with the back of Navy's head.

"Boy, stop staring at my woman. What the fuck is wrong with all of you? I'd swear none of you has ever seen a woman," Gunny commanded, glaring at the men around the table.

"Apologies, Gunny, I meant no disrespect, but you have to know your woman is fucking gorgeous," Navy muttered sheepishly, rubbing the back of his head.

Banging the gavel on the table, I brought the meeting to order.

"Right, we all know why we are here. Beverly, welcome officially to the Crow MC family. Please ignore the children. They'll eventually stop staring."

"Thanks, Reaper. I appreciate the welcome," she answered with a smile.

"Can you tell us what you know? I understand from Gunny that you have some information we can use as blackmail?" I asked.

"Yes, I do."

She pushed the envelope she'd brought with her down the table.

"You may want to brace before you open that up," she warned.

I sighed, wondering what can of worms I was opening by looking at this information.

Pulling the photographs out, I saw different men. Some I recognised from the tabloids and newspapers as the wealthy of London, and others were from the government. Some I didn't recognise at all. They were all in compromising positions with what looked to be minors. There was also a burner phone with copies of the pictures.

The last one I looked at was of a man with a young naked boy tied down over a desk in what looked like a home office. I saw the hate in the boy's eyes in the photo. This child was different from the others in that his cheeks didn't have a hollow look from not having enough food that the others had.

I'd handed the pictures down the table for everyone to look at. There were sounds of disgust as they each looked at the depravity of the men.

"Fuck's sake, these men are pigs. This girl doesn't look more than twelve," Bull muttered angrily.

"They need to be put down," Dragon seethed.

"They do, and they will be dealt with," Beverley agreed.

When the last one made its way back to me, I looked up at Beverly.

"Tell us about the pictures. I recognise some of the big names but not all," I ordered, passing the pictures back down to her.

Shuffling through, she pulled out the ones we would recognise and made a pile in front of her.

Holding up each one for us to see as she answered.

"These two are in the Home Office. These are in the NCA. This one is a real peach. He likes to make the girls hurt. He's a judge."

She threw the photo into the middle of the table.

"That's why he's gotten away with stuff for so long."

"Fuck. How are we going to stop any of this? We can't just take them out. Too noticeable," Draco grumbled hoarsely, rubbing his hand over his chin.

"You're not. I am," Beverly corrected him in a hard flat voice.

"Babe," Gunny protested softly.

Beverly turned to him, resting her palm against his cheek.

"I have to, honey. I know the man best, and he isn't going to expect the attack from where it will come from. Trust me, we have thought this through. It can't go on. He needs to be stopped. He and his cronies are rotten to the core. We don't need them in government or public services. The MC can't be involved as much as it wants to be. If you're caught with all these crooked men in power, none of you will ever see the light of day."

Gunny sighed and pressed a kiss to her palm before nodding and saying, "Well, fill us in on the plan."

Smiling at him, Beverly stood with her hand resting on Gunny's shoulder for support. It was clear from her pained expression that this wouldn't be a pretty story.

"I'm going to stay standing for this if that's okay, and I think I need to start at the beginning so you can understand why I trust the people that are going to bring him down. The one that will eventually be his downfall will be this brave fourteen-year-old boy and his father," she said, tapping her fingernail on the photo of the naked boy tied to the table.

"Let me explain from the beginning. I was born and brought up in the same estate your foster kids are from," she explained to Reaper.

"I had a shit Mum but an awesome Dad. He was only sixteen when I was born, and although I lived with my Mum, he was always in my life, much to her disappointment. I always knew I could count on him. Gunny was one of the few friends that stuck around when I was born and was the only one there when he died in a bike accident when I was fourteen.

"Without him, life got hard. Mum was a drug addict and alcoholic. I knew the only way out of that life was to get qualified in something and get a good job. So I put my head down, worked hard, and finished school with good grades on my GCSEs. I went to college and did Business Management. I won't bore you with all the details, but long story short, I got a job in London at the age of twenty and thought I was made.

"I was so young and so fucking stupid. I caught the eye of Thomas R Worthington, the Managing Director of Worthington Shipping. By twenty-one, I was no longer working, and he'd put me in a flat as his mistress. I knew he was married, he didn't make a secret of it, and his wife knew about his affairs.

"I didn't care. I was young and, like I said, stupid. He wanted me. He paid attention to me. I was in a paid-for flat. I had food, designer clothes and more drugs than I wanted or needed. It didn't matter if he liked to get a little rough every now and then. I was tough. I could take it, I told myself. He always showed up with a bauble or two, a sweet apology, and that was that, until the next time."

I don't think she realised she was crying until Gunny handed her his bandana. She looked at it in surprise before smiling softly at him and wiping her face.

"This continued for a couple of years until one night, we were at a party hosted at Thomas' house. There was another man there, I didn't know him, but he seemed to know me. Thomas called me to the library and said I had to be nice to him and keep him happy. Unbeknownst to me, this meant I had to sleep with him. He left us there, locking the door behind him. It was then that it hit me what this was. I'd heard rumours that Thomas sold women, but I'd never seen any evidence of it. The man was a lot stronger than me. No matter how hard I fought, he took what he wanted. He told me he'd paid good money for me and liked it when I fought. It was the longest four hours of my life. He left me broken and bleeding on that library floor. I crawled into the attached bathroom, and that's where she found me."

"Who?" Dragon asked softly.

"Maura Worthington, Thomas's wife. I'd heard things about her but had never paid it much mind. It was always bandied that it was a shame that poor Thomas married such a plain and ugly woman when he could have had anyone he wanted. What they didn't know was that Maura was the one that had the money, and he married her for it.

"That man didn't deserve her. She's an angel married to the devil. She picked me up off the floor, cleaned me up and was nothing but kind.

"She didn't have to be. She knew who I was. When I truly looked at her and saw under the makeup she had caked on the leftover bruising, I knew she was probably the only one who understood what I was going through. We became friends that night. I didn't see Thomas for nearly a month after that, and by then, I'd found out I was pregnant with Alec.

"Before you ask, I know he's Thomas' because the guy who raped me used condoms. Plus, if you see Maura's son, there is no doubt.

"Thomas insisted I get an abortion. When I refused, he kicked me out. Maura and I had kept in touch, and she helped me leave London. It was hard, but I got clean. Alec and I made a life for ourselves in that shithole estate. I worked when I could but mostly managed with the money, I made from the jewellery I sold and the benefits I was entitled to.

"When Alec was about three, Thomas decided he wanted to see him. There wasn't much I could do to stop him. He was clever, though. Whenever he came around, he brought just enough drugs to leave me wanting for the next hit. Before long, I was back in the loop. With me checking out, Alec started running wild and was getting attention from the local cops. Maura contacted me to say that I needed to reel him in. She'd overheard Thomas saying he would come to take him. If that happened, I knew I'd never see him again.

"Just to be clear, this was before I realised he had a penchant for young boys. I still didn't want him anywhere near my son.

"I found Gunny and asked for his help. He didn't have to help me. I know he did it initially because of my dad. I didn't hide anything and told him everything. We arranged that it would look like Alec was killed in a hit-and-run. Gunny knew someone who could help with the paperwork. We got a new birth certificate showing Gunny as Alec's father. He moved schools, and Gunny put that he'd been home-schooled until then. I explained everything to Alec and why he needed to keep it secret.

"I love my boy. It's the one thing he has always known. The plus to all this was he hates his father. He'd seen how he treated me from a young age. And he was thrilled to be working with Gunny. By this time, I was nearly thirty-five and assumed I was too old, and Thomas would lose interest."

Taking a deep breath, she sighed, wiping her eyes, "Unfortunately, he didn't."

"One night, I went to sleep in my shitty flat and woke up the next day in a flat in London. It was one of several that Thomas owned, and they were full of girls and some boys whose bodies he sold to whoever paid the most. He didn't care what condition they came back in as long as he was paid. It was sickening.

"The first year, he kept me drugged up, and I'm sure Gunny thought I'd dropped off the face of the earth. By the second year, he weaned me off enough to sell me, and by the third year, he had me on just enough drugs that I was functioning and running his whorehouse. How I didn't end up with a life-threatening disease, I don't know.

"It was when young girls and boys started disappearing, and the bodies were found in the Thames or some further north that it penetrated the drug fog enough. I began to do something about it. I started to wean myself off the drugs as much as I could and still function. It's fucking hard to find just the right balance. I didn't want him and his cronies to realise I was sober. They don't hold back on conversations when they think you're stoned. That was how I found out about this young man," she said, tapping her finger on his photo again.

"I contacted Maura and hoped she'd be able to help. She was only too happy to get out of her marriage, but the only way she could was to find a way to put him away for life or kill him. He'd had her sign her entire inheritance over to him after she'd had Todd by threatening his life when he was a baby. She'd known he was serious when she found him in the nursery holding a pillow over their son's face. He'd told her he would make it look like she had done it if she ever thought of leaving him. He needed her pedigree and the contacts her family name offered.

"We started plotting. It was purely by accident that she stumbled across John in that photo. When she realised what was happening, she took photos. John saw her do it. He approached her afterwards to ask what she was planning to do with them, and when she told him, he offered to help in any way.

"Turns out Thomas had threatened to use his younger sisters instead if he didn't comply with having Thomas use him once a week. They were twelve and ten. On that phone, you'll find a recording of a conversation between John and Thomas to that effect. Where Thomas fucked up is that John's father works for one of the biggest newspapers in the UK. Or maybe he's so arrogant he just doesn't care. Who the fuck knows what goes on in his mind.

"I reached out to Gunny because I'd recognised some of the lab addresses when they were talking, and I knew it would cause issues in the village. Thomas is arrogant and doesn't think anyone would dare take him on. I got what information I could to Gunny, who got me out and into rehab.

"You lot bombing the labs and dropping one of his men at his house has him running scared, and he's starting to make mistakes. His men are jumping ship like the rats they are.

"Monday nights are the nights that John goes to his home office. Tonight he is going to get a surprise because this afternoon, John told his father everything, and Maura handed over all the evidence we gathered to John's father. Tomorrow you should start seeing arrests happen. John's father has far-reaching contacts and is very angry, especially after listening to that recording.

"I'm sorry he isn't going down for the drugs, but he will be for the rest. Maura said she'd call as soon as she could. So it's just a waiting game now."

Beverly sank down onto Gunny's lap, exhaustion clear on her face after telling us her tale. He pressed a kiss to her forehead and wiped the tears that were running down her cheeks.

I thought we were all a little stunned at the story she had woven. There was no way we would have realised the hornet's nest we'd have stepped in if she hadn't done what she had.

"You're a fucking strong woman, Bev," Thor said, tapping her knee. "Got any sisters?"

She started laughing. It was just what was needed.

"Okay, let's wait to hear from Bev's friend Maura. I want to say thanks for stopping us from biting off more than we could chew. A drug gang and one guy in parliament we could have handled but the clique he had? Not so much. I think we would have been screwed and probably would have ended up in prison."

There was muttering of agreement around the table now that we all realised this group of animals' reach.

Needing to get the night over and wanting to go see my Dad to update him, I ended the meeting,

"Right, meeting adjourned. Let's have a beer."

I banged the gavel, and there was a rush to get out. I think we all needed to clear our heads. I collected all the photos lying on the table, put them back in the envelope, and went over to where Bev and Gunny were still sitting. I handed her the envelope.

"You can do what you want with this. Welcome to the family."

I pressed a kiss to her forehead and was rewarded with a small smile. I tightened my hand on Gunny's shoulder before leaving them.

Stopping at the door, I turned to them and said with a small grin,

"No fucking on the table, old man."

Gunny barked out a laugh, "Fuck off, Reaper."

I left them then. I knew Bev would need to decompress. I headed to the bar to have a beer with my brothers.

CHAPTER 13

ONYX

I didn't think any of us knew how to feel after the bomb that Beverly dropped on us. We all knew we'd dodged a bullet. We probably all would have ended up in jail or worse if she'd not handled the situation for us. I didn't much care about the ACES not going down for drugs because what they were going down for was far worse. Selling and using children was beyond evil.

The next few weeks, we watched as it all unfolded and arrests were made. The shock of it all ran the length and breadth of the country. And I knew that it would be years until it was all resolved. The one good thing was that we knew child molesters didn't last long in prison, no matter who or what their connections were.

We'd continued to do recon on the sites we'd blown up to see if anyone was attempting to set up shop again, but so far, nobody had been back to them. However, the village was slowly coming back to life, and the pub was doing well. The bouncers reported that they hadn't seen any drug dealing going on in the car park.

The women had been talking about holding a fair of some sort to get the community back together. They'd be bringing it up at the next meeting after doing some research with the rest of the shops in the village. They were thinking of having it in about six weeks' time at the end of July, the weekend before the school holidays started.

As for Rea and me, we seemed to be stuck in a status quo situation where neither of us wanted to rock the boat. We were still sharing a bed; it was both heaven and hell. Heaven, because it's my first peaceful sleep in years. I loved having her next to me and waking with her wrapped around me. The hell was that I woke up hard every morning. I was spending a helluva lot of time in the shower in the morning.

As for Mila, my heart was already gone for that little girl. The way she lit up and held her arms up to be picked up when I walked into the room. I was the one she wanted when she was tired. Not even Rea could settle her down. The way she snuggled into me when she was ready to sleep melted my heart.

I didn't think my heart would take it if Rea wasn't open to us trying again and kept Mila from me.

For now, I'd continue as we were. I knew the day was fast approaching when we'd have to make a decision. And as much as I wanted to, we couldn't keep on in this limbo that we had going for much longer.

CHAPTER 14

REA

It had been a long couple of weeks. Onyx and I had been getting on fine, and he adored Mila, and she adored him right back.

I knew that we needed to clear the air about our history. I was reluctant to rock the status quo we had achieved, but he had the right to see where his son was buried and the pictures that I'd kept.

Decision made, picking Mila up from where she'd been playing on our bed, I went and found Maggie to see if she would watch Mila for me for a couple of hours. Heading to the kitchen first, as that was more than likely where she would be.

"Hi, Maggie," I said as I walked into the kitchen. I settled Mila in the high chair next to Maggie, gave her a handful of Cheerios to keep her busy, and set her cup of water within reach. At nearly a year old, she was more than happy to feed herself.

Maggie smiled at us from where she sat at the table, peeling potatoes, more than likely for tonight's supper.

"Hello, love," she replied before turning to Mila, kissing her little hand, and getting a wide grin.

"Can I ask you a favour?" I queried a little hesitantly.

"Of course, love. What do you need?" she answered instantly.

I bit my lip as I looked at the wonderful woman who'd stepped up as an adoptive grandmother to my girl, and in all the time I'd known her, she had been there to support and hold us up. I felt tears fill my eyes as I thought of the loss of not having her in my life these last six years.

Inhaling a shaky breath, I looked at her, and I could see she knew what I would need without me even asking.

"It's time, isn't it," she said softly, wiping her hands on the hand towel on the table.

"Yeah," I replied. "We need to put it to bed, or we're never going to move forward. Either it will be together, or we may decide that it hurts too much and call it a day."

Maggie stood and put her arms around me, pulling me in for a tight hug and pressed a kiss to my cheek and said softly, "Whatever happens, if you both decide not to give each other a chance, the only thing I ask is that you and this beautiful little girl don't disappear from my life."

Stepping back, she let go of me and wiped under her eyes before saying, "Now, he should be at the clubhouse with the others. They had Church this morning but should be done by now. Go find him and get this settled. Mila and I will be fine. I'm going to get all this in the slow cooker, and then little Miss and I will take a walk in the buggy as the sun is shining."

I nodded and gave my baby girl some love before heading out the back door, only stopping to pull my boots on. I looked up just as I was about to leave to see Maggie talking to Mila and my baby answering in her baby babble. I smiled as I turned to leave the house.

Heading over to the Clubhouse past the cottages and about a five minute walk up the road. It was the first time I'd seen all the renovations they had done to the barn. The double doors were standing open. Due to the heat, I guessed. It was a pretty warm Spring Day. I could hear the hum of voices the closer I got.

Stepping through the door, I waited for my eyes to adjust before looking around. It was so different to when we had camped there growing up.

There was a comfortable seating area with sofas, armchairs and tables on the left. To the right were pool tables and a couple of dart boards with rubber matting on the floor. Just past them was a beautiful wooden bar. Behind the bar, Cairo was serving Abby, Noni and Avy. The men must still be in Church, I thought, making my way to the bar.

"Hi, Rea," they all greeted me as I walked up.

"Do you want a drink?" Noni offered.

"No, I'm good, thanks," I replied with a smile.

The double doors into the barn opened, and the men came walking out laughing and joking. Onyx was laughing at something Rogue had said, then jumped on him, getting him in a headlock while the others were grinning at the two of them joking around.

Noni made a little sound, and I dragged my eyes away from the men to see Avy and Noni with tears in their eyes as they watched.

"It's been a long time since Onyx has been like that," Avy explained, waving her hand to the roughhousing men.

The men realised we were watching, stopped messing around and stood up. I could see when Onyx noticed me standing with the women because his dark gaze latched on to me. He went quiet, letting Rogue go.

Reaper headed straight for Abby, laying a hot kiss on her, making Avy groan in disgust and punch him in the arm. Their laughter faded into the background as Milo got closer to me.

He stopped right in front of me, his dark gaze troubled.

"Is it time?" he asked softly.

I nodded and looked up at him.

"It is. Your mum is going to have Mila for us."

He sighed and ran his hands through his black hair. I could see he wanted to have this conversation as much as I did, but I thought we'd both feel better once we cleared the air.

"Okay," he said, taking my hand and leading me to the door.

I was very aware of the silence that we left behind us. I could only hope that what we discussed didn't break us completely.

As we made our way to the family parking lot, we didn't say anything. Then, as Milo went to take us to one of the vehicles, I stopped him.

"Can we take your bike?" I asked softly.

"If that's what you want," he replied and opened a bag on the shelf where the helmets were kept. Pulling out a helmet, he handed it to me, and I felt my eyes well up with tears when I realised it was the helmet he bought me when he turned nineteen. It had my name etched in blue down the sides.

Sniffing a little, I took it from him and settled it on my head as he started his bike. Then, when he was ready, he held his hand out to me, and I climbed on behind him, wrapping my arms tight around him. It was tough with a broken arm, but I managed.

"We need to go to my place first to pick something up. I'll tell you where to go after that," I told him.

"Okay," he agreed and pulled out.

We stopped and waited for the Blaze to open the gate, and then we were through and on the main road to the village.

I'd forgotten how freeing it felt to be on the back of a bike. It wasn't long before we were pulling into my driveway. I hopped off and took off my helmet. I pulled my keys from my pocket.

"I won't be long," I said to Milo before opening my door.

I knew exactly what I was looking for. Heading into my bedroom, I opened the wooden trunk at the bottom of my bed and pulled the blue box out of the trunk, leaving the pink box behind. I wrapped the box in a scarf and headed back out the door. I put the box in the bike's saddlebags, took my helmet from Milo and got back on the bike.

"Head into the village until we get to the traffic lights. I'll direct you from there," I told Milo, getting back on behind him.

"Okay," he said, pulling away from the house.

I could tell he was worried about how the conversation would go, and there was nothing I could do to ease his worry until we'd had it out.

Once we got to the traffic lights, I directed him where to go, and I could feel him tense under my hands as we entered the children's cemetery.

Directing where to park, I got off the bike and handed him my helmet. Once he was standing next to me, I opened a saddlebag and removed the box I'd put in there, cradling it to my chest.

I started walking towards where our son was buried and realised he wasn't following me.

Looking over my shoulder, I saw him standing by the bike, his shoulders hunched and his chin tucked into his chest.

Walking back, I took his hand in mine, saying softly, "Come, Milo. It will be okay."

He gripped my hand tight as we made our way through the headstones. I stopped in front of a black granite headstone with a blue motorbike engraved. Under that was the name *'Gabriel Milo Davies'*, then the date of his birth and death and the words *'Beloved son. Born Sleeping. Ride Safely. Until we meet again, forever in our hearts.'*

The man beside me started to sob as he read the gravestone. I wrapped my arms around him and held on tight as he finally realised all that he'd lost.

"I'm so sorry, Rea. If I could go back in time, I would do it all differently. I'd never have put us both through the last years of hell. I'm sorry for everything I've put you through and the loss that you've had to handle by yourself. I'm not sure how you could ever forgive what I put you through. I'm not sure I deserve forgiveness."

He openly wept.

My tears ran in rivers down my face as I listened to him beating himself up. I tucked my cheek against his chest, and I accepted our loss for the first time in six years. I held and listened to this big, strong man break, and my heart broke all over again for the both of us and what could have been.

At that moment, I forgave him for breaking us, and I acknowledged that I'd played a part in our break-up. I had blindly believed a woman whom I knew hated me. I knew he was going through a bad time after losing most of his team. Instead of accepting the word of a woman who hated me and the photos I'd been shown, I should have confronted him or spoken to one of his brothers or cousins. Never again would I take anything in our relationship for granted.

He'd always held the key to my heart, and I hoped that after today we could start building our relationship again stronger than before. The foundations were there, if a bit shaky. They just needed shoring up and strengthening.

When he finally fell silent, I lifted my head from his chest, cupping his cheeks. I took in the devastation showing in his eyes. Then, standing on tiptoes, I pressed my lips to his, and they clung to mine for a second before he released me.

"Come meet your son," I said softly, sitting on the grass in front of our son's grave.

Patting the ground next to me, I pulled on his hand and waited until he sat next to me, legs crossed, before lifting the lid from the box on my lap.

Right on top was a picture of Gabriel and me after I'd given birth to him. I passed it to Milo. His hands shook as he took the photo from me.

"He was beautiful," he whispered.

"He was," I said, handing him another photo of Gabriel wrapped in a blanket this time.

In another photo, I showed him the footprints and handprints the hospital did for me showing exactly how tiny he was.

"It's my fault you lost him. No wonder you hate me. I hate me," he muttered brokenly.

I sighed a little, holding his hand tight. I wiped away the tears with my other hand before replying, "No, babe, you aren't to blame. I know I made it out like you were, but you aren't. It was just easier to blame you. The truth is I went into early labour. I was just over twenty-two weeks. The doctors did all they could to stop it, but nothing worked. It was just one of those sad things. It's more common when carrying twins, but it can happen to anyone. There are some that think it can happen because of stress and anxiety, but it's not conclusive.

"I was under a lot of stress at the time, doing long hours at the hospital training and not looking after myself as well as I should. I hadn't let anyone know I was pregnant, not even my flatmates. I wanted to tell you first. What you did may have added to the stress, but it was just timing. It could have happened the week before or three weeks later. Nobody knows."

I rested my head against his shoulder as we looked at the pictures of our son before I continued.

"I did fall apart afterwards, and it was bad. I couldn't pull myself out of the dark pit I'd fallen into, and it was easier to blame you for everything. I was at my lowest when I did this," I said, pulling the leather cuff off my wrist without the cast. He'd seen my scars before but hadn't said anything.

"My flatmates found me and got me to the hospital, where I got the help I needed. But what really pulled me out was my mum getting sick. I had to help Dad. I was worried that I would fall apart again when they passed away one after the other, but I didn't. I had the tools to keep me going.

"It was around then that I met my ex-husband. He was a local multi-trader. I hired him to get my parent's house ready for sale. We hit it off, and he made me laugh."

Milo let out a slight huff at my words. I nudged him slightly with my shoulder, he twined his fingers through mine, and I continued.

"In hindsight, we never should have got married. I didn't feel for him what he felt for me. It wasn't right to him. We tried for two years and finally realised we were better as friends. He said he was tired of fighting a ghost that was still alive. And encouraged me to make contact with you because he didn't think I would ever be happy until we'd resolved our issues.

"He's now happily married to someone I introduced him to three months after our divorce."

After I told him all of this, Milo was silent for a minute before saying quietly, "I'm sorry your marriage didn't work out, Sugar. I don't know how I'll ever make it up to you. But if you decide I'm worth the risk, I'll work every day to make sure you know that you and Mila are my priority. You'll always come first. I also promise I won't ever keep secrets from you unless you tell me you don't want to know. I love you. I've always loved you.

"When I found out about your engagement, I went a little nuts, and I wasn't careful with my life. How I didn't get killed, I will never know. It was like someone was watching out for me. Maybe it was our boy because I should have been killed several times while out there.

"It was only when I was told about your divorce that I calmed down. I think everyone drew a breath of relief once they realised I no longer had a death wish.

"That night I saw you at the club, I can't describe how I felt just being in your presence again. And then, when you told us about Mila, my heart sank. I thought you were with someone and missed my chance to make my mistakes right with you.

"Dragon came back from dropping you home and proceeded to beat the shit out of me. I didn't try to protect myself. I deserved every punch he laid on me. When he told me you weren't seeing anyone, I felt hope again, then with the ACES causing so much destruction, I didn't want to bring you into it.

"You were right calling me out about that. I was a coward. I was scared you would push me away. When I got that call from you when you'd been beaten, my heart stopped, and I knew I couldn't keep away. Even if nothing ever happened between us, I needed you close so I could look after you and Mila."

He pressed a kiss to my head, his fingers tracing over the small feet and hand prints before continuing.

"You sharing my bedroom has been bittersweet because if I hadn't been an arse, you and Mila would have always been there. I would have experienced every aspect of your pregnancy with you. I would have felt her moving in you. That night you allowed me to help you bathe, and I couldn't stop staring. You are so beautiful. Your body is different from the last time I saw you naked. This time showing battle scars from growing and carrying not one but two children. I was so proud of you for doing it all on your own. If you knew how hard it was to keep my hands to myself that morning," he said gruffly before turning his head to look at me with heat in his eyes.

I couldn't resist. I pressed my lips to his. Before retreating, his mouth parted with a moan as he licked along the seam of my lips. I shifted to my knees to have better access to his lips. Wrapping my arms around his neck as he pulled me onto his lap. His mouth left mine but not before he pressed another soft kiss to my lips.

We spent the next couple of hours talking, wrapped up in each other next to our son's grave, and nothing had felt more right than this did at this moment.

CHAPTER 15

ONYX

It had been an emotional day. We'd left the cemetery after we'd cleared the air, and Rea had assured me she'd forgiven me and had explained that she was just as much to blame as I was.

I couldn't help but still feel an overwhelming feeling of guilt at how I'd treated her. It would be a long time before that feeling went away, and I vowed to take each day at a time and work my arse off to never make her feel that way again.

We stopped in the village as I wanted to buy a frame for Gabriel. He didn't deserve to be in a box. Rea had explained that it had been too painful for her to look at his picture but that she was ready now. We chose a silver frame with Baby Boy written across the top and framed his photo and his foot and handprints. We'd ridden home with her arms wrapped tight around me and my hand on her leg. I needed to be connected as I was still feeling raw.

I helped Rea off the bike when we got home, and she waited while I walked the bike into the garage. When I was done, she took her helmet off and shook her hair before tossing it back over her shoulders.

I couldn't resist her as I walked over. I threaded my hands into the hair on the back of her head and tilted her head back before lowering my mouth to hers, running my tongue along the seam of her lips until. She opened for me. I kissed her hungrily, not sure if I would ever get enough of her now that I had her back in my arms.

Wrapping my other arm around her hips, I pulled her in tight, rocking my hips against her. She let out a gasp as I deepened the kiss. Her arms wrapped around me and pulled me tighter into her body. Rea let out a little whimper. She tasted so good, a long-forgotten dream.

Lifting my head, I released her lips, and her eyes slowly opened, hazy with need. I couldn't help myself lowering my head again to dive back into another hungry kiss before lifting her up. Her legs wound their way around my waist, and I pulled her tight against me. I walked her over to the garage wall, pressing her up against it. Hungrily I rocked my hips against hers, so deep in the memories of what had been that I was only dimly aware of the sound of a bike entering the garage behind us.

Only when the deeply amused voice of Rogue penetrated the sensual haze did we pull apart.

"Don't mind me," Rogue drawled, his voice filled with humour. "Although not much privacy here, brother, and the kids will be pulling in from school soon. Not sure if Abby would appreciate the girls getting an education on the birds and the bees just yet."

Rea let out a squeak at the sound of his voice and buried her face in my neck.

His voice filled with laughter at Rea's reaction.

"Just saying."

"Ugh, shut up, Rogue. Way to clam jam a girl," Rea muttered, removing her head from where it was buried against my neck and glaring at Rogue.

I shook with laughter at her words, as did Rogue.

"Clam jam." He howled with laughter. "Rea, you kill me."

"Hey," she grumbled as her feet hit the floor, and she pushed me away.

Her hands hit her hips as she glared at Rogue, still sitting laughing on his bike.

"Do you know how long it's been since I've had sex? And as I don't have a cock it can't be cock blocker, so it has to be a clam jam. Fanny blocker just doesn't have the right ring to it," she grumbled, wrinkling her nose in disgust.

Still laughing, I grabbed the bag with Gabriel's photo in it, wrapping an arm around her shoulders. I pulled her close and pressed a kiss to her temple.

"Come on, babe, let's go check on our girl. Once we've done that, I'll see what I can do to alleviate that dry spell," I said, urging her on past Rogue, who was still chuckling as he got off his bike.

Rogue was right. The garage was not the place to get caught in a sexual haze. My only excuse was that it had been so long since I'd had her that I wasn't thinking straight.

We headed to the kitchen to find Mila sitting on the table in front of Mum, playing with play dough. She squealed happily as soon as she spotted us and started bouncing on her little butt, clapping her hands and babbling, "Mama, mama,".

Rea went still before a big grin broke over her face, and she shot over to Mila and scooped her up.

"Hello, baby girl. Who's so clever."

She smooched kisses all over Mila's face making the little girl giggle and squirm until she saw me over her mother's shoulder.

With hands opening and closing, she held her arms out for me, "Da da,".

My throat choked up, and I had to wipe my eyes when I heard her words. I plucked Mila from Rea's arms and held her tight to my chest, pressing a kiss to her head before lifting her high in the air above my head.

"Who's being such a clever girl today, saying words?"

It was just what was needed after a day like ours. This beautiful little girl with those few sounds had healed the wounds in our souls.

Cradling her to my chest, I wrapped my arm around Rea, pulling her into our hug. Lifting my eyes, I saw my mum with her hands clasped in front of her mouth and tears in her eyes, watching us. Motioning her forward, we pulled her into our hug.

We heard Ellie shout from the backdoor, "Yeah, group hug."

I braced myself, knowing what was coming just before she hit the back of my legs.

I let the women in my life go as I turned to see Ellie's grinning face looking up at me.

"You fixed your broken," she shouted, jumping up and down and clapping. "Your colours are blue. No more black."

We watched in amusement as she danced around the kitchen until she got back to Abby's side and stopped.

"Can I have a snack, Momma A?"

I snorted with laughter, and pretty soon, the whole kitchen was filled with laughter. It seemed food was far more important to Ellie than Rea and me fixing our broken.

As it should be.

As much as I wanted to take Rea straight upstairs and spend the evening in bed with her, I knew it wasn't going to happen. Parenthood responsibilities took first place for us. I could wait. I figured we'd waited years. A few more hours wouldn't matter.

We were sitting around the dining table finishing up supper when Reaper banged his hand on the table to get our attention.

"A little bird told me there's no school this Friday?" he said with a smile as Ellie shrieked in delight.

"Really, Pop, there's no school?"

She giggled happily, bouncing in her seat.

Suddenly she stopped and narrowed her eyes at her dad before sputtering uncertainly, "You're not lying, are you?"

Reaper shook his head and grinned at her, "When have I ever lied to you, squirt? No, I'm not lying, and as it's going to be nice and sunny, I thought we'd go to the beach for the day. The whole family. We're closing the businesses and having a family day. I think we all deserve it."

The whole table erupted. I sat back and watched as Noni, Kate, Abby, and Avy narrowed their eyes at Reaper, who just shrugged his shoulders.

"We all deserve a break after the last couple of weeks. You don't have to close, but you can if you want."

"We'll get cover," Noni said, looking at the other women who were nodding. "You're right. A day at the beach sounds great."

"Dad's being released tomorrow, and it was his idea. He's sick of being inside and wants a day of fresh air," Reaper informed us.

That was amazing news. I would be glad to have Shep back in the fold.

I leaned into Rea and whispered in her ear, "Are you ready to go upstairs?"

She tilted her head and slanted her eyes up to mine, nodding with a small smile.

"Yeah, can you bring Mila? I'll meet you up there. I'm just going to grab her bottle."

Standing, I helped Rea out of her chair before picking Mila up. I knew there was no way we would be able to leave quietly. It had become a nightly ritual where she was passed around getting good night hugs and kisses.

When she was back in my arms, I snuggled her close and headed upstairs to get her ready for bed and her bottle so I could have time with my lady.

CHAPTER 16

REA

Standing in the kitchen waiting for Mila's bottle to warm so I could take it up to her, I couldn't help but feel nervous about what I knew was coming. It had been a long time since I'd been with anyone. I guessed I could be glad he'd already seen me naked. That was one less thing for me to be nervous about.

I headed up to our room and stopped in the doorway to watch them as he got Mila changed for bed. He only had her night light on and was murmuring softly to her. Her gaze was fixed on his face as she listened to him.

"Your mum's the love of my life, Mila. You are the second-best thing to ever happen to me. I'm going to work hard every day to make sure you and your mum know you are mine to love, hold, and protect. So do your old man a favour, and don't be interested in boys until you are at least thirty."

Mila babbled something back at him, and he nodded his head, his face serious.

"You agree. That's good, baby."

He finished with the last popper and picked her up, snuggling her into his arms. He headed to the rocking chair in the corner of the room and settled down before holding his hand out to me.

"Look, Mummy is here with your bottle. Let's get you fed and into bed, so you can sleep and grow."

I walked over to them and took Mila from him when he handed her to me, then settled on his lap when he pulled me down on it. He held us as I fed Mila her last bottle, and I couldn't help but tear up a little. For me, this was my perfect dream. Milo, me and Mila as a family.

We sat like that for a while, content to be together. When Mila was fully asleep, I stood and settled her in her cot before holding my hand out to Milo and pulling him into his bedroom.

The only light was the moon shining through the open curtains and the faint light from Mila's night light through the crack in the door.

Stopping by the bed, I pulled my t-shirt over my head, leaving me in nothing but my jeans, bra and panties. My fingers went to the button on my jeans, but Milo stopped me with a hand on mine.

"Let me," he whispered.

He then pulled down the zipper, popping the button, before pushing the denim down my legs as far as they would go before kneeling in front of me. Milo lifted each of my legs out, kissing the inner thigh as he removed the denim.

Left in nothing but my panties and bra, my breaths were coming faster as he stayed on his knees in front of me. I could feel his breath on my pussy and let out a shaky breath when I felt his lips on me. I knew I was wet. I could feel myself soaking my panties.

He pressed a hard kiss to my centre before he pulled my panties down, and I stepped out of them. His hands gripped my thighs as he lifted one of my legs over his shoulder.

I was open to his gaze.

Looking down, I watched as his dark eyes flicked up to me as his tongue wet his lips. I moaned when his tongue swept my folds. Threading my fingers into his hair, I tugged gently. He didn't disappoint as he swiped over my clit with his tongue.

I shuddered in response.

Gripping my hips in a firm grasp, he pulled me tight against his mouth and thrust a finger into me. Between his mouth on my clit and his finger pistoning in and out of me, it wasn't long before I could feel my orgasm rolling through me.

I threw my head back and whimpered his name as I came, "Milo."

Just as I thought my legs wouldn't hold me up anymore, with one last swipe of his tongue across my clit Milo rose and crushed his lips against mine as he devoured my mouth.

Tasting myself on him sent me into a frenzy, and I attacked the hem of his shirt, trying to get it off him without removing my mouth from his. Finally, he helped me and stripped it off. While he did that, I grappled with the button of his jeans.

Pushing my hands away, he picked me up and placed me on the bed before stripping hurriedly and joining me. Pulling my bra down under my breasts, he sucked and nipped until I squirmed and hissed with need.

"Now, Milo, I need you now," I pleaded as I pulled him over, wrapping my legs around his waist.

We both stilled as he entered me. As soon as he bottomed out deep inside me, he dropped his head into my shoulder, grinding it gently against me.

"Fuck, baby, you feel so good. It's been so long."

He lifted his head from my chest and looked down at me. He tilted his hips back and then pushed forward. I tilted my head to the side and felt his lips as he pressed a kiss to my neck, making me shiver.

"I don't think I'm going to last, Sugar. You feel too good," he growled into my ear as he pushed forward again.

"Then don't," I whispered back.

Pushing up until he was on his knees, he moved my legs from around his waist to over his left shoulder, making our fit tighter. His eyes didn't leave mine. Taking his thumb, he sucked it into his mouth, then he pressed it to my clit before powering into me with hard thrusts. He was hitting that spot inside me with each powerful thrust, and just as another orgasm flowed through me, I felt him tense as we came together. He kept gently thrusting until we both finally stilled.

I let out a happy sigh and got an answering smile in return. Pressing a kiss to the calf of the leg closest, Milo then placed my legs gently on the bed as he slowly pulled out of me. I let out a whimper as I felt him leave me.

"I know, Sugar. I'll be back," he murmured softly before heading to the bathroom.

I heard him running water, and then he was back with a cloth. He cleaned me before heading back to the bathroom. I sat up to take my bra off just as he came back in. Getting into bed, he pulled the covers over us. I snuggled into him, my head pillowed on his shoulder.

"Rea, I'm sorry. I didn't think to use anything. I'm clean, babe, and I haven't been with anyone in over two years."

"I trust you, Milo. I know you would never do anything to put me in danger, so I didn't say anything. I've got an IUD, so I'm good on the pregnancy front, and I haven't been with anyone in over four years," I replied with a yawn.

"Okay, then," he said quietly, holding me tighter before pressing a kiss to my head.

"Love you, Milo," I muttered tiredly.

"I love you, too, Sugar. Sleep. It's been a long day."

That was the last thing I heard before I let sleep take me.

CHAPTER 17

MILO

The morning sun hitting my face woke me as it came through the bedroom window, making me grumble. I opened my eyes to see we'd forgotten to close the curtains before falling asleep. Looking at the alarm clock beside the bed, I saw it had just gone 5 a.m.

It was then that yesterday hit me, and I turned my head to look at the woman curled on her side in the bed next to me, her hair spread over our pillows, her face soft and peaceful in sleep.

I reached out, moved a piece of her hair from her cheek, and tucked it behind her ear. Her nose wrinkled, and her eyelashes fluttered a little before she opened her eyes. I watched as the sleep cleared from her eyes, and she smiled.

"Morning," she whispered, her voice husky with sleep.

"Morning, Sugar."

Moving, I rose above her before lowering my head for a kiss. Her arms came around my shoulders, holding me to her. Turning onto her back, she pulled me with her, and I settled between her spread thighs, my already hard cock nudging her silken heat. With a whimper, she tilted her hips and tightened her thighs around my hips, pulling me into her hot, wet sheath. I stilled as she moaned and rocked against me. My mouth trailed from hers, down her throat to her breasts, sucking one of the puckered tips into my mouth.

I was rewarded with a warm gush around my cock. Groaning, I stopped my hips from thrusting into her. I wasn't ready to come yet. I moved onto her other breast, giving it the same attention before making my way back up to her mouth.

I thrust my tongue into her mouth at the same time as I pushed my cock deeper into her. Stopping and waiting for her to adjust, when I felt her pussy clench around my cock I started to move, thrusting my hips in time with my tongue in her mouth.

Before long, her pussy was fluttering around my hardness. She ripped her mouth away from mine with a cry as she clenched around me. It wasn't long before I followed her and came harder than I'd ever come before. I rested my cheek against her breasts as our breathing evened out.

Rea was running her fingers through my hair. It hit me then how much I'd missed this, missed her. As my softening cock left her body, the emotions I was feeling were too much, and my breath hitched as I tried to fight the sadness at how much I'd missed out on with her.

"Shh, Milo. It's done. No more looking back from today. We're going to be okay."

Lifting my head from her breasts, I looked into her beautiful green eyes, seeing nothing but love in them.

I softly pressed a kiss to her lips before nodding.

"You're right, Sugar. We'll be okay, and if I'm ever that stupid again, just have Dragon shoot me."

"Huh, not likely I'll shoot you myself."

She grinned at me.

Then nudging me with her hips, she asked, "Want to join me in the shower before Mila wakes up?"

"Hell, yeah," I said, getting up and out of bed before picking her up and throwing her over my shoulder. It made her laugh, and she hit my arse with her hand as I walked us to the bathroom.

I made sure she was clean and then proceeded to dirty her up again before Mila made it known she wanted breakfast. We hurriedly got out of the shower and dressed, laughing all the while. I was finished first and went and picked our daughter up out of her cot, got her dressed and ready for the day.

If this was my future, I couldn't be happier.

CHAPTER 18

ROGUE

Friday had arrived, and Ellie had us up with the sparrows wanting to head to the beach. Abby had managed to calm her down and had her help pack cool boxes and bags with enough food, drinks and snacks to feed us for the next week, never mind just for that day.

I'd kept my mouth shut after hearing Aunt Kate tear into Draco when he'd wanted to know if they were expecting an apocalypse. She'd told him she didn't want to listen to whining from grown men that they were hungry, so he'd better shut up, or he wasn't getting fed at all today.

He'd shaken his head and headed to the garage with the other men.

I'd finished my coffee and gone to put my mug in the dishwasher when I was met with my aunt's narrowed eyes.

"And you? Do you have an opinion on anything this morning?"

I'd grinned at her before replying, "Only that you look amazing this morning, Aunt Kate. Having Shep back looks good on you."

She flicked the dish towel she held in her hand at me and laughed.

"You smooth talker, go on get out of here and tell the prospects to come and load these cooler boxes into the vehicles."

Pressing a kiss to her cheek, I hightailed it out of there before she changed her mind. I found the prospects and had them head into the house to help bring out the food.

The parking area was chaotic, with everyone milling about and talking loudly. Shaking my head at the madness, you'd think we'd never been to the beach. I headed to my bike and checked the saddle bags to make sure I had a towel, an extra t-shirt, shorts and flip-flops. Skinny and I had ridden the route earlier in the week to scout out a place to set up on the beach. I was happy we were leaving early because trying to find enough space for all of us on a crowded beach wasn't going to be easy. I was hoping it wouldn't be too busy, with today being Friday.

I cracked up when I heard Ellie's piping voice say impatiently over the voices in the parking lot.

"Pops, you need to give them orders. They're taking too long. Daylight's a-wasting and the beach is calling my name."

There was stunned silence before everyone started laughing. I turned from my bike when I heard Shep's booming laugh. It was good to have him back, even if he wasn't at full strength yet. Ellie was standing in front of Reaper, her little hands on her hips, her head thrown back, and her eyes narrowed on her father as she watched him laugh. She started tapping her foot when he continued to chuckle, and when she crossed her little arms, I knew she was getting serious. Reaper must have as well because he bent and picked her up, pressed a kiss to her cheek and apologised.

"Sorry, baby girl. You're right. Let's get this show on the road. Do you think you can whistle like I showed you?"

"Yeah, I can. But, you better close your ears," Ellie advised with a hint of a grumble.

Her scowling face showed her displeasure at us not taking her seriously. I was with her, though, and wanted to get the show on the road, so I threw my leg over my bike and settled down, waiting for the signal. I didn't have to wait long. Ellie put her fingers in her mouth and blew a high-pitched whistle that had most of us cringe, but it got the job done and everyone's attention as they turned towards her.

"Load up, my girl has spoken. Let's hit the beach and grab some breakfast," Reaper ordered.

There was a mad scramble as everyone that wasn't riding loaded up into vehicles. The rest went to their bikes.

Reaper and Abby pulled up to the front near me. As Road Captain, I would be leading the ride.

Draco fell in just to Reaper's right. Onyx, with Rea on his bike, was to his left. The rest fell in behind them, with the prospects that weren't driving vehicles bringing up the rear.

Pulling out of the manor's gate, we headed to the main road out of the village. The ride would take about an hour. Looking in my mirror, I saw all my brothers behind me with the vehicle carrying the kids, my aunts and Shep following us.

The emotion I felt as I watched to ensure that all was well with everyone settled something in me. I'd been feeling restless now that the drug issue seemed to have cleared up and Shep was out of danger. I'd been toying with the idea of asking

Reaper if I could take some time and go AWOL for a bit. I knew he'd understand my need for freedom. I was a restless soul, and my brothers got that about me.

The effects of my mother leaving us landed differently with my sister and me.

Noni was a homebody and never left the village if she could help it. It was almost as if she had to prove she could be relied on and would never leave.

I, on the other hand, got jittery if I stayed in one place too long. The itch to travel had got stronger over the last couple of days. But for now, spending time with my family and taking this ride would have to do.

My thoughts must have consumed me because when we rode into the parking lot by the beach an hour later, I hadn't noticed the time that had passed while riding.

I walked my bike in and waited on it as Abby got off Reaper's bike so he could park next to me.

It was already heating up, and I couldn't wait to get out of my leathers and into something cooler. We waited for those who were travelling in the vehicles to park and get out. We didn't have to wait long for Ellie to bounce out of one of them. She was fairly vibrating with excitement as she waited for us.

Remembering how hard it was to be patient at that age while everyone got settled, I quickly stripped my leathers off until I was standing in my shorts and T-shirt that I'd worn under them.

"Hey, Ells," I called to her, "Grab your towel, girl and let's hit the waves."

She gave a shout of excitement.

"Thanks, Uncle Rogue."

Then she dashed off to Abby to get a towel.

I stowed my gear in my saddle bags, grabbed my towel and hat and met Ellie by the stairs that led to the beach. They were stone, set wide apart smooth in places from continued use over the years, and covered in a fine layer of sand.

The beach was pretty quiet as we'd got here so early that the crowds hadn't arrived yet.

She grabbed my hand and bounced down the stairs next to me, chatting nine to a dozen. I grinned as I listened to her tell me that none of the others in her class was going to have a great day at the beach, and she couldn't wait to tell them all about it on Monday. She kicked her shoes off as soon as we hit the sand and took off towards the waves but got sidetracked on her way there.

Stooping, I picked up her shoes and went to follow. As I rose, I saw a sight that had my breath hitch in my chest. Ellie had stopped and was chatting with a dark-haired beauty. I could see by how they conversed that they knew each other. While she was busy listening to Ellie, I took the opportunity to study her. She had long dark brown hair in a braid, the end resting just above the curve of her backside. She had a Rubenesque shape, with wide hips and thick thighs. As she turned to brush the whisp of hair that had escaped her braid back from her eyes, I felt my dick go hard at the full lushness of her breasts where they pressed against her t-shirt.

Fuck.

The woman was everything that I found attractive.

Slim women were beautiful too, but I'd leave them to other men.

Me, I liked the feel of soft flesh around a woman's hips that I could sink my fingers into and a firm rounded arse that I could feel as I pounded into her.

The thought of those lush thighs wrapped around my hips had me licking my lips and cursing softly. I pulled the towel I'd wrapped around my neck and brought it around to hold in front of me to hide my hard dick.

Hearing a chuckle to my right. I turned to see Draco out of the corner of my eye, smirking at me. I'd been so enthralled by watching the woman that I hadn't realised the others had followed us down and were now setting up.

"See something you like, brother?" Draco asked with a grin.

"Fuck, yeah. Who is she?" I asked as the older kids stopped and talked to her.

"She's a teacher at the secondary school," Reaper answered from where he'd stopped next to me. "Her name is Julia Walker, and she's the one who's been helping the kids with uniforms and stuff until we took them in."

Reap looked at me. The expression on his face showed he wasn't bullshitting me when he said, "She's not a plaything, Rogue. You go there, make sure it's serious. She's going through some shit at the moment and has taken some time off school to help with her Dad. He's terminal.

She's not the type you play with. She's the type you make an Old Lady."

"I can see that Reap, and I have no intention of just playing. Seeing her hit me like a ton of bricks, and I didn't even know who she was. Now that I know I'll go slow," I answered him seriously. "Do you think I can get one of the women to introduce me?"

"You won't need to," Milo said, bumping me with his shoulder and pointing.

I looked up to see Ellie dragging Julia towards us. Next to me, Reaper chuckled and grinned at me.

"That girl will have all the brothers matched before long."

"Uncle Rogue, this is Ms Julia. Your colours match," Ellie announced before she dropped Julia's hand and took off back towards where the rest of the family were setting up.

The men around me chuckled, but my attention was taken by a pair of shy dark eyes framed by arched brows and thick lashes. Her face was bare of makeup, not that she needed it. Her olive-toned skin had a tinge of pinks across her softly rounded cheeks that flashed with deep dimples as she smiled a shy, uncertain smile offering her hand to me.

She murmured softly, "Julia."

Taking hold of her hand, I squeezed it gently.

"Rogue, but you can call me Marcus."

Her eyes flashed in surprise at me giving her my first name, before they turned to the men standing next to me and greeted them.

"Reaper, Draco, Onyx, it's good to see you."

Draco grinned flirtatiously at her, and it took everything in me not to punch him in the face. But it seemed my woman was immune because she didn't bat an eyelid when he laid it on thick and drawled out, "Julia, looking as gorgeous as ever."

Her eyes narrowed slightly before she turned her back on him and said to Reaper, "Katie was just telling me that you are thinking of arranging a fair over the summer. Be sure to let me know, and I'll see if I can get the school involved."

She chatted a bit more and seemed comfortable around the brothers she'd met when they'd been on school pick-up. But it wasn't long before she was making noises about leaving.

"Are you sure you can't stay for a bit?" I asked, not ready to let her go just yet.

She shook her head and said regretfully as she pulled her car keys from the pocket of her denim shorts, "I can't, I'm afraid. I need to get back to the hospice."

"Well, at least let me walk you back to your car," I urged, taking her gently by the elbow and walking her to the steps.

She turned and waved goodbye to my family before smiling at me again and started climbing the steps up to the car park. We carried on walking in silence until we reached a red Ford Fiesta. It was old, but it looked like she kept it in good condition.

She cleared her throat nervously, and I cut off the groan that threatened to escape as I watched her tongue run across her lips.

"Well, this is me," she motioned to the car.

"So it is," I agreed.

Taking the keys from her hand, I unlocked the car and opened the door for her. Helping her in, I slotted the keys in the ignition before pulling the seatbelt across her body. I smiled a little as I heard her breath hitch when I brushed against her hip as I snapped the seatbelt in place.

Pressing a gentle kiss to her cheek, I murmured, "Drive safe, baby."

I retreated and stood up. Julia touched a hand to her cheek as she looked at me with wide stunned eyes.

I grinned at her before waving and sauntering back to the stairs, where I stopped to watch as she pulled out of the car park.

I couldn't wait until the next time I saw her. Reaper was going to have to put me on school collections, so she could get used to seeing me. I could tell she was not sure by my attention, and I wondered why.

This Crow man has found his lady, and I was not letting her get away.

CHAPTER 19

ONYX

We'd had a good day at the beach with the family and had spent a lot of it taking the piss out of Rogue and his fascination with the hot teacher. His words, not mine.

I could already see where this was going. It wasn't just a saying. It really was true when a Crow man met his match. We knew right away.

I'd known at the age of fourteen when Rea had walked into our classroom. Reaper had known when he'd met Abby, as had our parents.

Thor said he knew his ex wasn't his one. Gunny had said his first wife had been and that he hadn't expected a second chance until he met Bev as an adult. I could see that the guys not from our family and the prospects thought we were crazy.

They'd see.

The ride back had felt right, and we'd all enjoyed relaxing into it and the freedom of all being together without the stress of the drugs and Shep being in the hospital hanging over us.

We'd pulled up into the yard just as the sun was going down. Parking up, I tapped Rea on her knee in a signal to dismount. I walked the bike back and parked it next to the others switching the bike off.

I pushed down on my cock as it hardened as I watched Rea take off her helmet and shake out her hair before tossing it back over her shoulders. When she unzipped her jacket, her breasts pushed up against her t-shirt all the while talking to Abby about the day.

Getting off my bike, I wrapped my arm around her shoulders and pressed a kiss to her head. Smiling at her, I got an answering one in return.

"Why don't you head up, Sugar? I'll get Mila and bring her up for bed."

Standing on her toes, she pressed a kiss to the corner of my mouth before agreeing.

"Okay, baby, see up there. Night Abby."

"Night, Rea, see you tomorrow," Abby replied before she headed to where Reaper was pulling Ellie out of the car.

I grinned as I listened to her from where she was snuggled against Reaper's chest, her eyes heavy with sleep, but it hadn't stopped her from talking.

I followed them upstairs with Mila asleep in my arms and listened to their conversation.

"Best day ever, Pops. Thank you for taking us."

"You're welcome, baby girl. Glad you enjoyed yourself."

"I love our family, Pops. I'm glad you chose us. I never want to leave you and Mamma A."

"And you won't if Abby and I have any say in it. You're our girl."

"And Bren and Ben?" Ellie asked sleepily.

"And Bren, Ben, and Sam, you're all ours."

"Good. And soon, we'll have Ms Julia, Rea and Mila too."

I chuckled, listening to her. I was pretty sure if Reaper let her, she'd list us all off.

"Yeah, you think?" Reaper asked.

"Mhmh," Ellie hummed. "We're all family, and when you and Mamma A have a baby, we'll have even more love."

This girl, everything was so simple for her. As far as she was concerned, she was safe and loved, which was enough for her.

We'd hit the top of the stairs, and I was going to be turning toward our wing but not before I said goodnight to this precious girl.

Cupping my hand on her head, I leaned over and pressed a kiss to her forehead.

"Night, Ells, sleep tight, baby girl. I'm glad you had a good day today."

"Night, Uncle Onyx, I had the best day. I can't wait to tell my friends on Monday, but now I'm going to sleep."

Still chuckling, I headed down the passage to my wing, calling softly over my shoulder as I left, "Night Reap."

"Night, brother."

The lights were on dim as I entered the room and headed to Mila's nursery.

My stunning woman was waiting for us, a little sunburned no matter how much sunblock she'd used. Her eyes showed her fatigue but were soft and happy when she turned from the dresser as we walked in. Rea had fresh pyjamas and a bottle waiting for Mila. Laying Mila down, we made short work of getting her ready for bed. I left the two to enjoy some time together while Mila drank her bottle and went to the bathroom to shower.

I'd just got in when the shower door opened, turning my head and watching as Rea got in. Pulling her into my arms, I smiled when she automatically tightened her grip on me and laid her head on my chest, the water beating down on both of us.

"Tired, baby?" I questioned softly.

"Yeah, but it's a good tired. We all had so much fun today. I missed your family, and I'd forgotten how much they loved messing with each other. The new guys fit right in. Poor Rogue, you guys took the piss out of him today."

I chuckled, "We did, but he can handle it, and I think Julia is just the woman for him. Maybe if he's shacked up, he won't be so restless and want to leave all the time."

"Oh, hunny, he's always going to be restless. But you are right. With Julia having a job at the school, he'll only be able to take off at certain times of the year. It's going to be interesting to watch that one play out. She won't make it easy for him."

"Good, he needs to work for it. Women usually just fall at his feet. Enough of my brother. I have you naked in my arms, and I've had to watch you run around in your black bikini all day and baby, you are sexy as fuck when you get competitive playing Frisbee. Although next time, wear a shirt. I wanted to punch several guys today," I grumbled, pouring her shampoo into my hand and rubbing it into her hair.

She giggled at my comment and then groaned as I massaged her head. I knew she loved her hair being washed, but I was so hard I could pound nails into a wall with my cock.

Adjusting the shower head so that the water ran down on us, "Rinse your hair, Sugar," I instructed, licking my lips as her breast lifted when she raised her arm, the water running over her pert breast.

Bending, I latched on and sucked hard at her turgid peak, hearing her gasp as I moved on to her other breast. I swept my hands over her curves and across her back, pulling her closer to me as I ran my tongue up her neck to her ear, nipping at the lobe as she shuddered against me.

'Yeah, I knew my woman and all the spots that made her want me inside her.'

I tweaked her nipples hard as my mouth covered hers, catching the gasp that left her lips. Kissing her long, wet, and hard I cupped her pussy and smiled as she adjusted her legs to give me better access. It was my turn to groan as I felt how turned on she was. Thrusting my fingers into her, my thumb put pressure on her clit. I was leaking pre-cum against her belly and was desperate to be inside her, but I needed her to come first.

Removing my fingers from her, I got a grumble, making me chuckle. Adjusting us I pressed her back against the tiles, hearing her gasp at the cold against her back before I dropped to my knees. I pushed two fingers back into her, making a come-hither gesture and sucked her clit deep into my mouth. Her fingers dove into my hair and tugged me tighter against her. Rea started rocking her hips against my face, the walls of her pussy were starting to pulse around my fingers, and I knew she was close.

She came hard and fast with a sob and a wail.

I continued until she couldn't take it anymore and pushed my head away.

"I swear to God, Milo. If you don't fuck me soon, I might explode."

Standing up, I grinned at her as I sucked my fingers into my mouth, watching her eyes flare at my motion. Tucking my hands under her thighs, I lifted her and sunk my cock deep within her folds.

It was my turn to moan as her wet heat engulfed me, and I couldn't hold back anymore as I pounded hard into her. I came so hard my knees weakened. I held us up against the wall of the shower panting, my head buried into Rea's neck.

"I missed this," Rea said softly, her hands running over my back and through my hair.

"Me too, baby," I said. "But never again. You have me until we are old and grey."

"I can't think of anything better."

My legs steadier now, I let go of her legs and finished washing us. Which led to another round of lovemaking. This time I made it to the bed.

CHAPTER 20

TRICKSTER CAFÉ

3 WEEKS LATER

REAPER

It had been a quiet few weeks now that the ACES were over and done with. The fallout was huge, and the effects of what people in power had done would be felt for years to come.

Our businesses were thriving as the village came alive again. Summer was on its way, and we expected a fair bit of traffic to come through.

The women were going to have a huge fete on the farm we'd purchased next door to us. One of the fields closest to the main road had been allocated for it, and we had all been drafted in to make sure it was ready.

At this stage, we just agreed to whatever they wanted to be done. There was no way I would tell my woman or mother they couldn't have a carousel or hayrides. As far as I was concerned, they were running the show and could do what they liked as I knew fuck all about running a fete.

From Church on Friday evening, I knew that the tickets were almost sold. All the shops in the village were closed for the day, pointing people at the fete as they would all have stalls set up there.

Avy and Molly, who lived on the farm next door and owned a brewery, were combining forces and running the pub tent. Maggie and Noni were organising the catering tent. All of us men and the rest of the kids had been drafted into helping with parking, security, or being goffers.

The giving soul I was, I'd drafted in Liam and his lads to come and help. They were happy to lend us their services as all the moneys raised was going to help the local schools with the equipment they needed. Some funds were allocated to doing a facelift on the village high street, and the rest towards funding free self-defence classes at the gym for children from the local schools. Julia was working with the women on this as she was a teacher and knew who would benefit from it. She had arranged for volunteers from Year 10 & 11 pupils to run the face painting and glitter tattoo stall. And some of the lads that were friends with ours had volunteered to help with parking and setting up in the morning.

Even the local council had got involved and had arranged to have enough bathroom facilities delivered for the day.

It was the first time in a long time that the entire village was pulling together for the good of the community.

All in all, it created a lot of excitement, and it was a good way to start the summer holidays.

The planning of the fete was why we were all gathered in our café on a Sunday for early breakfast before it opened. We had a few council members, Julia and the Head

Teachers from the local schools, a few of the shopkeepers and Molly there for a meeting to finalise everything.

My hand was resting on Abby's lap, and every now and then, she'd squeezed my fingers, letting me know she was thinking of me before she continued talking and making lists on the notepad next to her plate. I'd finished my breakfast a while ago and was sitting back doing what I did best, watching. My eyes roved over my family, and I smiled as I took in the contented look on my father's face as he did what he did best... watching. I caught his eye and grinned at him getting one in return before we continued casting our eyes around the room, cataloguing expressions and seeing if there were any problems.

Hearing Ellie laugh, I smiled as I saw Sam teasing her and pretending to tickle her. Ben was grinning big as he watched them. The change in him had been huge since we'd taken them in. He'd shot up four inches in the space of three months, and being able to eat as much food as he wanted, he'd filled out no longer so thin that his bones were sticking out. He was also packing on muscle and never missed a session at the gym with Dragon and Carly.

It had taken him a long time to relax around all of us, but as the girls became more comfortable around us, he let go and just became a young lad. He was still the most responsible out of the three lads, but Alec and Sam had for most of their lives had an adult be the responsible one, whereas Ben and Bren had had to be the responsible ones in their family.

It was good to see Alec, Ben, and Sam forming the bond they had. Ben and Alec had taken a little while to get back to the friends they had been when they were younger, but Sam had helped smooth things over when things got tense.

My woman had done a fantastic job with her son. He was hardworking and easy-going. Nothing was ever too much trouble for him. He'd taken to being a big brother to the girls like a duck to water, and I thought this had helped Ben in a big way, knowing he was no longer the sole protector of his sisters.

My eyes moved to Bren, our shy, quiet, gentle, beautiful girl. I'd hoped she'd come out of her shell more, and she had but only in the comfort of the manor and our family. When we were in public, she still seemed unsure, and her gaze was constantly roving around as if looking for threats. We'd got her into self-defence classes with Carly, and she was progressing but cringed every time she had to hit anyone. Although she had no problem taking her frustrations out on a bag.

I wasn't too worried as when she was threatened, she was happy to punch whoever was bothering her, as Alec had learned when he'd snuck up behind her and given her a fright last week when she'd been practising on the bag at the gym.

We laughed when she turned and hit him before realising who it was. She'd been mortified and hadn't stopped apologising until I said, "Baby girl, stop apologising. You did what you've been training for. Alec just learned a lesson not to mess with you."

Alec had agreed.

"Reaper is right, Bren. This is why we are training. It's self-defence, and it's good that you didn't hesitate. I won't be sneaking up on you again, that's for sure. Good job."

She'd blushed from our praise, although I think that had more to do with Alec than me.

Bren, Bella, and Carly had their heads together and were discussing something seriously. Every now and then, they nodded and made notes in a book. I wondered what they were cooking up. I'd come back to that later. What I didn't like was how Alec was watching my girl. I narrowed my eyes when he caught me watching. Looking a little sheepish, he turned to Sam and started a conversation.

'Yeah, you keep your eyes off my girl until she's older.'

"We need to sort their situation out, Reap," Rogue muttered.

He'd caught me watching the kid's table.

"We do," I agreed. "If it doesn't get resolved soon, we'll discuss it without the women and get it done. There is no way they are ever returning to the situation we took them from."

"How're things going with your lady," I asked, grinning at him.

I knew it wasn't going smoothly. Julia seemed completely oblivious to my boy. It was a cause of great amusement among us, and we didn't let him forget it. It was good for him that he had to work for it.

He sighed as his eyes wandered over to the woman that had him tied up in knots, watching her chat with the rest of the women in our family, totally oblivious to Rogue and his attempts to flirt with her. He'd finally given up and sat next to me.

"Honestly, I have no idea what to do. She doesn't seem to realise that I'm interested. I've been going slow as I know her Dad is not doing well. She's back at school now, and I'll see her when I pick up the kids with Abby. She's always pleasant and friendly, but that's it."

"You need to woo her. After listening to some of her conversations with the girls she sounds like she has no self-confidence because of what society has deemed an acceptable size for a woman. Reading between the lines of those conversations, she's been used and let down several times. It's always been about her size," Dragon advises from down the table.

Out of all of us, he's the one that all the women and kids love and seem the most comfortable with. Even Julia was more open with him than any of us.

"There's nothing wrong with how she looks. She's gorgeous. I hate the media and what they deem is acceptable. Bloody heroin chic, I thought we'd got over those days," Rogue grumbled, looking a little pee'd off that Dragon seemed to know more about Julia than him.

Dragon grinned at him, "Preaching to the choir, brother, you know my taste in a woman is not much different to yours. By wooing her, I mean making her life easier for her, especially now that her Dad is in hospice. Have the women find out what she's up to. If her car needs a service, be the one to pick her up and drop her off. Pick up supper and take it to her one night a week so she doesn't have to cook. When you're at her house, see if anything needs fixing and offer to fix it. Woo her.

"She's been alone for a while, from what I understand, and is used to relying on herself for everything, so make sure she doesn't have to. Compliment her and not to get into her pants. Mean it. Notice things about her. Has she had her hair done? Does she look more tired than normal? Find out why. If you know she's going to be out late like she was the other night at the pub, offer to follow her home. You know she sees her Dad every morning and every night. Offer to take her. Just small things like that."

There was soft clapping from Rea across the table, who was sitting tucked under Onyx's arm. Since they'd got back together, they were never far from each other and always touching when they were in the same vicinity. It was great to have our brother back to what he'd been before he'd royally fucked everything up with her. She was also the only one other than our sisters who knew us originals well, as we'd all been in the same class. Rea was also the only one who still called us by our first names, although she had been trying to remember to use our road names.

"Milo, I always said that Drake was the most intelligent out of all your brothers."

She laughed softly, not wanting to draw attention from the other women, although I knew Abby had been listening from the beginning just from the way she'd leant into my body and had stopped writing in her pad.

"Drake is right, Marcus, sorry Rogue, you'll need to be patient with her. She's not used to being put first, and you had better be serious about her, not just messing around. She's been hurt a lot."

"I wish you'd all stop warning me about that. I know what she's worth. She's going to be my old lady just as soon as I can tie her down. I wouldn't mess around with her feelings. You should all know that. All the women I've been with have always known the score," Rogue ground out, looking pissed at us for questioning him.

I clapped him on the shoulder, "We know, brother."

Abby turned in her chair and looked around at Rogue, her brown eyes sparkling happily and said with a smile, "Don't worry, we'll help Rogue. I'll get together with the other women, and we'll come up with a plan. We like her. She'll make a good addition to our circle."

The tension seemed to seep out of Rogue when he realised he was not alone in getting Julia to fall for him.

Ten minutes later, the meeting broke up, and we'd cleaned up the aftermath. Everyone was milling around outside, intending to go for a ride, and the kids were waiting to be ferried back to the manor by Mum and Shep.

Bev had walked off when a phone call came in but now was walking back to us with a worried expression.

"Abby, that was Maura. She and Todd are on their way here and want to stop by to update us on what's happening in regard to the ACES. She called as a courtesy because she wasn't sure how you'd feel about her and Todd pitching up out of the blue. She doesn't want to upset you and will understand if you don't want to see them."

Abby tensed under my arm. Sam, who'd been standing behind us talking to Alec but had heard what Bev had said, immediately walked to her other side and slipped an arm around her waist.

She tilted her head back to look at him, "I don't mind what you do, Mum. He means nothing to me. You, Reaper, Ben, Alec, the girls, and the MC are my family, not him and not her," Sam assured her.

When she looked at me, her face and eyes showed her worry, but I also knew she needed closure because I thought there was more to him signing his rights away to Sam than she knew.

"Like Sam said babe, we are here for you. If you want closure, then this is a good time to do it. We are all here for you. You aren't alone anymore," I reassured her.

By now, all the Crows were gathered around us, listening to what was happening.

"Okay," Abby responded with a deep breath. "Tell them to come to the café, and they can meet us. But I'm telling you, Bev, if they even try to take Sam from me, they'll have a fight on their hands."

"Abbs, if I thought they were a threat to you even for a minute, I wouldn't have let them anywhere near you. I promise Maura isn't like that, you'll see," Bev assured before walking off and making a phone call.

Turning, I found Mum and Dad waiting by the Range Rover and said to them, "Can you take the kids home, so they're not here for this."

Surprisingly it was Ben that baulked at the request, "I'm sorry, Pops, but I'm staying with Sam and Mamma A. I'm not leaving them. We're a family and stand together no matter what is thrown at us. That's what you've taught us to do. But if we can put Ellie in the car, just in case things go sideways, that would be great."

My chest expanded with pride at my boy. He'd learnt a lot in the last few months. Abby left me to hug him.

"Thank you, Ben, and you're right. We are a family that always sticks together through good and bad. I think putting Ellie in the car is a good idea. You are right in case things get heated. I hope they don't but just in case."

I gripped the back of his neck and pulled him close, leaning my forehead against his.

"Proud of you, Ben."

"Pops, just doing what you taught us."

A soft voice interrupted us.

"I'm staying too. Mamma A has been good to us from day one. Sam has never made us feel bad for pushing into his family and sharing his mom. I'm not leaving them because it's easier than supporting them."

I took Bren into my arms and kissed the top of her head. "You kids make me proud. But I want you behind me and with one of the prospects, okay?"

"I can do that, Pops," Bren smiled up at me. "And don't worry, I think it will all be fine. Bev wouldn't bring someone around that meant any harm."

By now, the rest of the MC had realised something was happening and were standing to attention, much like we had in the military waiting on orders.

Lifting my voice, I explained what was happening and to be alert. Aunt Maggie got Ellie into the car and stood by the closed door with Dog, Mum and Dad.

"Skinny, you're on, Bren."

"Pres," he acknowledged walking over to Bren and pushing her slightly behind him. I heard her grumble something at him, but he didn't move.

"Okay, Bev, let them know they can come in."

She lifted her phone to her ear and spoke into it before hanging up.

"They'll be here shortly. They were parked down the way waiting for confirmation that they could come in," she said, looking at me.

It wasn't long before one of the new model Range Rovers pulled up into the back parking lot behind the cafe, where only family parked. The windows were tinted so we couldn't see in, which I wasn't happy about. We all stood tense and ready to move at a moment's notice.

The engine switched off, and the driver's door opened and out stepped what could only have been Sam's father, Todd. He was not what I expected at all. The last photo we'd seen of him was over ten years old. Where I was expecting a preppy-looking playboy, what stepped out was someone that could have been one of my brothers. He was as tall as me, with long blond hair he had pulled back, jeans, biker boots and a black t-shirt. His arms were covered in tattoo sleeves. Closing his door, he nodded at me before opening the back door and helping someone out. My attention was taken by the passenger door opening and another dude getting out. This one was just short of six feet six, dressed much the same as Todd, completely bald, and also covered with tattoos. He gave us a chin lift before leaning back against the grill of their vehicle with crossed arms. I didn't think he was nearly as relaxed as he let on.

My attention was drawn back to where Todd was now closing the door. I still couldn't see who he'd helped out, but whoever it was must have been tiny.

When he stepped aside and offered the woman next to him his arm, my eyebrows rose in surprise. This was his mother? She couldn't have been much more than five feet tall and didn't look like she weighed more than fifty kilos wet.

She was also dressed in jeans but had on sandals and a floral flowy top not much different to what I'd seen my mother wear. Her blonde hair was pulled back from her face, and she was smiling up at her son. When she turned back to us, there was a combined indrawn breath. The entire left side of her face was a network of scars going down the side of her face to her neck. Whatever had happened to this woman had been bad and painful. She pushed her sunglasses up to the top of her head as she surveyed us. When her eyes stopped on Sam, they closed, and she took a deep breath before walking forward. Bev broke away, walked up to her, and enfolded Maura in her arms, hugging her tight. The embrace was returned full fold. These women had a link that had been forged in fire and would never be broken. The fierce way they held onto each other told a story.

Bev finally let her go, tucked Maura's hand into her arm, and walked her to us.

She stopped in front of us, her eyes still wet with tears, before saying to me, "Reaper, I'd like to introduce you to my friend Maura. She's one of the reasons we're all standing here today."

I held out my hand and shook the hand offered to me, "Maura, it's good to meet you." I motioned to Abby, "This is my old lady Abby and our kids Sam, Ben, and Bren. In the car by my parents, aunt and uncle is our youngest, Ellie."

She turned to Abby with a smile, "Abby, it's good to finally meet you." She nodded at the rest of the kids, but her eyes lingered on Sam, and there was a sadness in them. She waved a hand behind her, "This is my son Todd, and over by the car is a friend, Roman."

Todd came forward when she introduced him and shook my hand, "It's actually

Cash. Only my mother and my old lady call me Todd now. And Roman is Maestro."

I shook his hand, and we eyed each other before we nodded.

He nodded at Abby, "Abby." Then his eyes moved to Sam, and he closed them tight and swallowed before clearing his throat, "Sam."

"Cash," Sam replied.

Abby had not said anything.

"Well, if this was a western, we'd be seeing a tumbleweed rolling through right about now with cheesy Italian music," Noni muttered. It was enough to break the ice, and everyone chuckled.

Someone, probably Thor, as he was the one who loved Spaghetti Westerns, whistled the tune for The Good, the Bad and the Ugly, making someone snort with laughter.

"I'd better not be the Ugly in that tune," Maura called out.

Yeah, it was him because he called out, "No love, Reaper's the ugly one."

I rolled my eyes, "No respect," but I was smiling.

Noni and her Dad had done what they did best and had broken the tension.

"So, Maura, what can we do for you and Cash?"

She pulled out several A4 envelopes from her bag.

"Is it okay if I hand these out to the relevant people?"

The top name was Sam's, and I tilted my head down to look at Abby, who still hadn't said anything. She nodded at me knowing I wouldn't do anything to upset Sam.

"Depends," I responded. "Is what's in those envelopes going to upset anyone?"

Maura tilted her head in consideration and looked up at Cash before shaking her head, "They shouldn't, but they may need some explanation that will be a bit uncomfortable."

Turning, I looked at Sam, standing next to me with Ben next to him, and Alec had moved up and stood just behind us behind Sam's back. I had a flash forward into the future and knew I was looking at the next MC President, VP and Sergeant at Arms.

"Sam?"

"It's all good, Pops."

I caught the wince on Cash's face when Sam called me Pops, but he didn't say anything.

Turning back to Maura, I nodded, "Go ahead."

With a deep breath, she took the top envelope and handed it to Sam, "In there, you'll find all the paperwork for your inheritance. You'll get some on your sixteenth birthday, some on your eighteenth and the rest on your twenty-first."

Sam went to hand the envelope back to her, "I don't want any of his blood money. We've done just fine without any help."

Maura gently stopped him, saying, "This isn't his money. This comes from my grandparents on my mother's side. It was always meant to go to Todd's children. This is your birthright."

"What about his other kids," Sam asked, looking at Cash.

Cash cleared his throat and replied, "They'll be fine. They have their own inheritance."

The two looked at each other, but then Sam said, "I'll accept it, but only if you apologise to my mother."

"Sam!" Abby burst out.

Cash held up a hand, stopping her. I tightened my arm around her waist and pulled her in tight to me. Bren broke away from Skinny, pushed up against Abby's other side, and burrowed in.

My woman was loved, and it was shown by our kids and the rest of the MC, who had moved closer when Bren had broken away from Skinny and bolted to her side.

"Sam's right Abby. I do owe you an apology. When you said you were pregnant, I panicked. I knew what my father was like, and there was no way I was letting him get his hands on my kid. So I did what I did best at the time. I lied and said there was no way it was mine. I went to my mother and asked for help. It was her that got the paperwork done so I could sign away my rights to Sam. I then publicly broke up with you and made it seem like it was because you were messing around and that the baby you were carrying wasn't mine. It was the only way to keep you both safe.

"Do I regret it? Yes. Watching Sam grow up from afar was hard, especially after my kids were born. I kept tabs on you as much as possible and threw work your way when needed. It was as much as I could do without my father getting suspicious.

"I left the UK as fast as I could when I hit eighteen to get away from him. He wrote me off completely when I joined The Wraiths, which was just fine with me. Then, I started working against him, stopping his shipments from getting to their destinations. We saved as many women and children as possible and started building a case against him. It's one of the reasons everything escalated so quickly because the authorities couldn't look away or hide the amount of evidence I brought with me.

"I owe you everything for bringing up Sam the way you did. He seems like a great kid, so thank you," he stated.

Abby's eyes grew wider and wider as Cash continued with his speech.

"Umm, you're welcome?" she responded.

I chuckled, and Sam just groaned, lowered his head and muttered, "Mum."

She smacked my stomach with the back of her hand when I chuckled and said, "Babe."

Moving out from under my arm with her hands on her hips, she glared at Sam and me.

"Well, what was I supposed to say? Thanks for knocking me up at sixteen, leaving me humiliated by our entire school, and going through a thirty-two-hour labour, mostly by myself, until the women in your family arrived and took control. But yes, he is an awesome kid, although not so much right now," she grumbled, still looking pissed.

I slipped my hand around the back of her neck and pulled her closer, leaning my forehead against hers, "You're right, babe. I'm sorry. I shouldn't have laughed. It was just how you said it, like you weren't sure if he was welcome," I said, pressing a kiss to her forehead.

She sighed and rubbed her face before turning and pressing her back to my chest and looking at Cash, smiling at us.

"Okay, they're right and thank you for your apology. Sam is a great kid, and Reaper's family have been with me since day one, so I was very lucky he's had, good role models. Just as well because I didn't have a clue what the hell I was doing."

"I don't think any of us do in the beginning," Cash said before turning back to Sam. "In your envelope is my number, my mother's number and numbers for each of my brothers. I know we are in the States, but if you ever need anything, call any of those numbers. That goes for you and Abby, too, Reaper. I'm forever in your debt. If you ever need anything, you just have to ask. I'm not going to force a relationship, but I want to get to know Sam when he is ready. I've also included pictures of my three kids with my Old Lady. They would love to talk to you."

Sam nodded and tucked the envelope under his arm before replying, "Okay, I'll think about it."

"No pressure. Only if and when you are ready," Cash reiterated.

Maura had been quiet up until now. When she saw Cash was finished, she added in, "That goes for me too, Sam. When you're ready, I'd like to get to know you."

She then took the next envelope and handed it over to Alec, "This is yours. I know your mother did everything she could to keep you safe. This is your legacy. It's clean money. I sold the business and divided the shares between my four grandchildren and you. Your mother is one of my best friends, and I consider you one of mine no matter how you came about."

Shock was on Alec's face as he turned to Bev and Gunny, who both nodded at him. Turning back to Maura, he cleared his throat and answered, "Thank you. I appreciate it and all you did for my mum while she was in London."

"You're welcome, Alec, and like Sam, you have a list of numbers in your envelope to use if you ever need us for anything," Maura continued before taking the second to last envelope. Walking over to Bev, she stopped in front of her holding it out.

"This is yours," she put shaky fingers against Bev's lips when she went to protest.

"I sold the house, got cash for it. That house had awful memories for both of us, this is your half. You saved me just as much as I saved you. That night I found you. I was ready to end it all. Todd was out from under the devil's thumb, and after he did this by messing with my brakes," she motioned to the scars on her face, "I didn't think I could go on. But finding you made me realise I was stronger than I ever imagined, and realising I could take him down made me stronger. So, this is yours, and if you ever need me, I'm just a phone call away. You will always be my family, no matter what."

By the time she was finished, both women had tears streaming down their faces, and there were a lot of moist eyes and throat clearing going on.

Bev pulled Maura in for a hug, and the two rocked together, "I'm going to miss you," Bev said tearfully.

Maura pulled back and smiled up at her before taking the tissue Thor of all people, handed her and then Bev.

"Thank you," she said, smiling at him. "You're welcome, love," he grinned back at her before ambling back and leaning back on his bike.

Looking a little flustered, she looked around at the group of us before replying to Bev, "I'm only over the pond, Bev. You can always come and visit. I'm going to stay with Cash and his family for a bit. We leave in the morning. Until I return, I'm only a phone call away if you need anything. Okay?"

"Okay," Bev agreed, leaning into Gunny, still tearful.

Maura came back to stand next to Cash, "Before we head out, I wanted to let you know there will be no blowback on any of you in regard to the blowing up of drug labs. The general consensus is that it was a gas leak," she grinned widely. "Well, several gas leaks."

"That's good to know. I heard the gas line was repaired and sorted," I grinned back at her.

Maura smiled before turning to Cash and saying, "One more thing before we go." Taking the last envelope, she handed it to Abby. "In there is the adoption paperwork for your three other children. Congratulations, Mom and Dad, you have a boy and two beautiful girls."

I was shocked.

"Maura, I'm not sure how you did it but thank you."

"What does that mean?" Bren asked softly.

Abby was wiping tears from her cheeks before turning and cupping Bren's face, "Baby, it means you're ours. No one can take you from us now."

Bren burst into tears and hung onto Abby for a while before she threw herself at Maura and hugged her tight.

"Thank you," she whispered into Maura's shoulder.

Maura lifted Bren's face from her shoulder and wiped the tears off our girl's cheek smiling, "You are welcome, sweetheart. Enjoy your new life."

Bren came back and burrowed between Abby and me.

Abby looked at Maura and then at Cash before saying, "Thank you, this means the world to us."

Maura waved her hand as if it was nothing.

"No thanks necessary. Get the papers to your lawyers on Monday morning. You shouldn't have any problems. If you do, call Cash or me."

Turning to Cash, Maura asked, "Do you have any more questions, or can we go?"

He shook his head and held his hand out to me, and then Sam,

"We're good to go. Don't forget, if you ever need anything, give us a call."

"Abby," Cash nodded respectfully at her.

"Todd," she grinned at him, slipping her arm back around my waist and burrowing close.

He just shook his head at her as he took his mother's arm after she'd done a round of goodbyes.

I gave a chin lift to Maestro as he stood up from the car he'd been leaning on and got one in return. We stood until their Range Rover disappeared from sight before we all drew a collective breath, and the tension eased.

I clapped my hands and turned, "Anyone still up for a ride?"

"Hell yeah," shouted back at me.

Turning to Abby, I asked, "Babe? Do you want to ride or head back to the mansion?"

She looked at Ben and Bren, who were now standing at the car talking to Ellie and my parents. They both just waved us off. She turned her attention to Sam to see what he had to say.

He smiled at her and waved the envelope, "Go for a ride, Mum, it's what I would love to do. I'll go through the envelope, and when we see the lawyer on Monday about the adoption papers, he can look through them. Enjoy the rest of the day. This doesn't change anything except make some things easier."

She grinned at me before pulling her helmet on, "Ride it is."

We waited until the vehicles were loaded with the kids and those not riding before we took off for a long roundabout route through the New Forest.

Today was a good day!

The End or is it?

EPILOGUE

CROW MANOR – 10 YEARS LATER

ONYX

The last ten years seemed to have flown by. I sat in one of the new cuddle chairs that Sam had built and added around the unlit fire pit. He'd said these would be more comfortable with the number of couples we had that wanted their partners close. And he was right.

Rea was lying back against my chest, her hands resting on her rounded belly that held our daughter. This baby had been a happy 40th birthday surprise. She was talking to Julia and Avy about the annual fair we'd held every year since the first one.

Hearing children's laughter and recognizing our eldest daughter's giggles, I looked over to see Julia and Rogue's eldest, Roman, chasing her and his sister

Rosie with what looked like a balloon filled with water. As it was a warm summer evening, I wasn't too worried about them getting wet. He was twelve, and they were eleven. Roman could have got them long ago. As he went to throw the balloon, he pretended to trip and dropped it by their feet.

The girls stopped and fell over on the grass laughing in delight, while Roman stood over them, grinning. He was soon joined by Reaper and Abby's son KJ for Kane Junior and Rea and my son Bobby named after my dad. I watched as they helped the girls up and grabbed a rugby ball and tags out of the sports cupboard we'd stocked up for the kids.

I knew it was coming before she made it to me. I could never resist my girl. I watched as she ran over, her long black hair flowing down her back, stopping by our chair as she hugged her mum before looking at me with her big dark eyes sparkling in a happy smiling face.

"Come play, Dad. I need you to whup their butts," she said, throwing her arms around my neck.

"You do, huh?"

"Yup, Rosie is getting Uncle Rogue and the others to come play too. We can have a proper game of tag rugby."

I saw my brothers coming over, some from the main house and some of the others from the clubhouse.

Pressing a kiss to Rea's head, I squeezed out from behind her, tucking a pillow behind her back and making sure she was comfortable. Then, rubbing a hand over her extended stomach, I pressed a kiss to it before lifting my head to look into my love's bright green eyes.

"Love you, Sugar."

"Love you too. Enjoy your game."

She grinned at me when our daughter groaned at us for being mushy.

"Come on, Dad. Hurry up, you and mum can kiss later," Mila grumbled, pulling on my arm.

Laughing, I picked her up, threw her squealing over my shoulder and ran to where the others were ready and waiting for us.

Life had been full of ups and downs like it had a wont to be in the last ten years. In all that, our family's constancy carried us through whatever life threw at us.

Right this moment for me was a perfect moment, and I knew by looking at my brothers laughing and joking as they chased our happy laughing children, they would agree with me.

NOW IT'S THE END

Bereavement Support Services

Child Bereavement UK – https://www.childbereavementuk.org/ - 0800 028 8840

Cruse Bereavement Care – https://www.cruse.org.uk/ - 0808 808 1677

Sands - https://www.sands.org.uk/ - 0808 164 3332

The Lullaby Trust - https://www.lullabytrust.org.uk/ - 0808 802 6868 - support@lullabytrust.or.uk

Acknowledgements

I would like to say a massive thank you to my Beta Readers Cloe Rowe and Clare. F. you ladies rock.

To my husband for always encouraging me on whatever crazy idea takes me at the time. Being there for me, always putting me first and for treating me like a queen. After 27 years you are still my inspiration.

My eldest daughter Helen offered positive quotes and comments daily during this journey. I love you more than the whole world and don't know what I would do without you and your encouragement. Love you, baby.

To my youngest, my lovely Ria, I love your snarky comments when we have to share the same space while I write. Don't ever change. Love you to the moon and back.

To my mum who keeps our house running smoothly, I honestly don't know what I would do without you. Love you.

To all my readers who took a chance on me with my first book Wild & Free and for reaching out with positive comments and suggestions.

One last thing .... **REVIEWS** feed an author's soul, and we learn and grow from them. Whether it be just a rating left or a few words they are what pushes us to keep writing.

About the Author

I grew up on a cattle farm on the outskirts of a small town in Zambia, Southern Central Africa. I went to school in South Africa, Zambia and finally finished my schooling in Zimbabwe. I had an amazing childhood filled with fantastic experiences. As a family, we often went on holiday to Lake Kariba and I feel very privileged to have seen Victoria Falls, one of the seven wonders of the world several times.

My grandparents lived on the same farm as my parents and me. It was my grandmother, my Ouma who first introduced me to the romance genre by passing her Mills and Boons on to me, and I was hooked from there.

I now live happily in Jane Austen country in the UK with my family, VA by day and wordsmith by night.

Follow me:

https://www.facebook.com/michelle.dups.5/

https://www.instagram.com/author_michelle_dups

www.michelledups.carrd.co

https://www.goodreads.com/michelledups

https://www.facebook.com/groups/837078130666476

Other Books by Author

Sanctuary Series

Sanctuary Book 1 – Wild and Free (Dex & Reggie)

Sanctuary Book 2 - Angel (Kyle & Lottie)

Sanctuary Book 3 – Julie (Julie & Joel)

Sanctuary Book 4 – Amy a Novella (Amy, Sean and Rory) Amy won't be coming out as a paperback due to its size. Instead, it will be as an extra in the back of Julie.

Sanctuary Book 5 – TBA

Crow MC

Reaper

Onyx

Rogue – April 2023

Draco – TBA

Dragon – TBA

Avy – TBA

Noni - TBA

Printed in Great Britain
by Amazon

26316432R00172